NEVER SAY NEVER

NEVER SAY NEVER

A Dedication to Love Beyond the Walls

A Collection of Poems and Short Stories

Susan Goins-Castro,
Rhonda L. Harris,
and
R.Y. Willingham

iUniverse, Inc.
New York Lincoln Shanghai

Never Say Never
A Dedication to Love Beyond the Walls

iUniverse books may be ordered through booksellers or by contacting:

iUniverse
2021 Pine Lake Road, Suite 100
Lincoln, NE 68512
www.iuniverse.com
1-800-Authors (1-800-288-4677)

This is a work of fiction. All of the characters, names, incidents, organizations, and dialogue in this novel are either the products of the authors' imagination or are used fictitiously.
All scriptures were taken from The Holy Bible King James Version except where indicated.

ISBN-13: 978-0-595-42109-1 (pbk)
ISBN-13: 978-0-595-86451-5 (ebk)
ISBN-10: 0-595-42109-1 (pbk)
ISBN-10: 0-595-86451-1 (ebk)

Printed in the United States of America

Contents

Acknowledgements

Susan Goins-Castro

First and foremost, I want to thank Almighty God for not only blessing me with the gift and talent of writing but for also giving me the strength and courage I needed to take a leap of faith by working on this beautiful project.

To my two co-authors, this has been an amazing journey that we embarked on. I have learned so much from you during this process. You both are truly amazing women. I can't believe that a year ago, we started out with just an idea and ended up with this. I am so proud of the finished product and most of all; I treasure the new friendships that have come about because of it. Let's do it again.

To my wonderful husband, you are the love of my life. Thank you for all your endless support and constant encouragement to follow my dreams. I couldn't have done this without you. You are my soul mate and my best friend. I love you baby, now and always.

To my beautiful children, I love you more than life itself. You are the reason and my purpose for working as hard as I do. You bring so much joy into my life even with all of our fighting. (smile). Always know how much Mommy loves you.

To my parents, thank you for giving me the gift of life and a wonderful one I might add. You have showered me with a lifetime of guidance and an abundance of love. I love you dearly.

To my family and friends, thank you for all of your support. And a special shout out to my cousin Malinda Love. "Just trying to make it" LOL You are the sister I never had. I love you gurl.

This is dedicated in loving memory to my amazing mother Barbara B. Goins who in spite of all my mistakes never told me that I was a disappointment to her. She was a prime example of beauty inside and out. I love you and miss you deeply.

Rhonda L. Harris

Giving thanks to God, The Father is my ultimate praise. He has faithfully guided me on my life journey and never turned away from me. I am thankful for the gift of love and all of the blessings that He has bestowed.

I am most grateful to my co-authors on this project. We have shared our love stories, our writing and our lives. What began as a spur of the moment idea of mine has resulted in not only this our finished work of love but also the development of lifelong friendships.

I am indebted to the love of my life who is not only the inspiration for my words; but also for my life. Thank you for introducing me to the world of *"Queen Dom".* Thank you for always upholding me to the level of divine esteem. Thank you for always loving me.

Many thanks and blessings are extended to my daughters who have made this journey with me yet they never questioned nor complained. Mommy loves you beyond measure.

I am thankful to my family and friends who have always supported me and accepted me and my decisions without ever judging me.

I am grateful to my favorite teacher who has impacted my life in ways more than he could imagine or even know. My high school English teacher, Mr. Saunders, was the teacher that everyone dreaded to have; but I loved him. He forced us out of our shell of comfort into a world of growth. He encouraged use to take every work we read/studied and make it entirely our own. He taught me how to breathe life into every work that I crafted. He taught me to use care and concern in every endeavor. He showed me the significance of leaving every situation in a better state than how you found it. He taught me not just how to write, but he also taught me how to live.

I am grateful to all Black Women who have maintained their voice of expression while sustaining their dignity and self respect. I have love and admiration for you all.

R.Y. Willingham

I am ever so thankful for my Lord's loving and perfect care. In you, I know that nothing is by accident or coincidence. I trust you fully.

I am blessed to have encountered two women that I really enjoyed developing our friendship. Our project has been a labor of love, with lots of laughter along the way. I wish I could bottle all of that creativity; it's a road to prosperity for us.

To my son, who taught me first to be a mommy, and then to be his mommy. I love your desire and drive. Watching you reminds me that we can do anything.

To my Magic Man who taught me the value of love. I am grateful for your patience. You will always be my lion—fierce, protective, strong, wise, and courageous. I got papers on you too!

Collective
Acknowledgment

Our friendship and collaboration on this project was initialized through our meeting online through the wonderful support community of Prison Talk Online (PTO). We are most grateful to PTO for providing a service for its members who have loved ones incarcerated or have re-entered society. *Never Say Never* afforded us a beautiful opportunity to acknowledge, affirm and express the power of these committed relationships.

Every team needs special players to offer the best of their gifts and talents. We want to thank Chandra Sparks Taylor of Taylor Editorial Service for her editing, suggestions and proofreading to enrich the expression of this book.

People come into our lives for a reason. We recently had the privilege of meeting and getting to know Nikki Barjon. She is among the leading female African-American publicists in America. Her energy, creativity and prowess are phenomenal. Nikki is not only our publicist but more importantly a valued and trusted friend. We are truly thankful for the immeasurable help and guidance she has provided to us.

Prologue

"Love is a many splendored thing."

—Sammy Fain and Paul Francis Webster

It was never our goal or intent to fall in love or be in love with a confined man, but what is one to do when love overtakes you? You follow your heart where it leads you. In our case, the channels of love lead us to a place behind metal bars and cement walls.

Loving a confined a man means beholding the *strength* of an Amazon, the *faith* of Job, the *will* of Malcolm X and the *heart* of the fearless and yes, we do possess them all. "For everyone to whom much is given, from him much will be required; and to who much has been committed, of him they will ask the more." (Luke12:48 NKJV).

Loving a man in prison embodies love yet separation; things both good and bad. Our relationships demonstrate the many splendored things that are coupled with love. Love, faith and commitment are tantamount to loving a confined man. This romance requires you to be committed to loving the man above, beyond and through the pressures of society, the demands of your family and friends and the never-ending criticisms from them all.

Devotion to our men in prison has not always been an easy task. Not because these men possess some character flaws that make them undesirable, unlovable and unforgivable as the media loves to portray. The uneasiness of our affair lies in living it out loud within a system that is not designed to sustain and nourish what destiny has brought together.

These words are a glimpse into our journey through fiction narratives that depict our stories of devotion to men in prison. This labor of love is dedicated to our loved ones who remain incarcerated. It is our gift to them. It is our gift to you. So come and step into our world of neutralizing love; and behold our flowers that bloomed in the moonlight.

She is the love of my life.

The air that I breathe.

My reason for continuing to push on every day.

She gives me hope and lets me know that regardless of the outcome, she will be there to love and support me.

Because of this, I give her the gift of my love ….

—*Geo*

My Gift to You

Susan Goins-Castro

To reach up to the stars at night and swing across the sky,

That's just one thing I dream to do before the day I die.

If I could buy those stars I see and tie them with a bow,

They would be my gift to you as you deserve them so.

With face and eyes as beautiful as yours and the joy you bring to me

With little talks that help one out, my wife you'll always be.

At times it's hard to say such words to a person in my sight

But the words I wish to say to you are in the sky at night …

As a little girl resting in my bed at night, I thought of my knight in shining armor. He was always tall astride that beautiful black horse. He gleamed late into the night as my perfect dream while I drifted off to sleep. In this dream, I would hold a tiny white box encapsulating a small bottle that enclosed nothing visible to the naked eye. My future love for my knight was in that bottle. It was as necessary as the air I breathed. I couldn't recognize it on sight, but when I inhaled and basked in its presence, I knew it by connection. Never in my wildest dreams did I imagine my love resting years later behind razor wire and guarded fences. As certainly as I had never imagined that, I recognized love in that tiny bottle in the air I breathed. He never was on top of that horse, and the gift he was to present to me was such a fortunate surprise.

This is my story of falling in love with Julius and receiving my greatest gift of all. It was my reversal of fortune.

—*Naomi*

Reversal of Fortune

R.Y. Willingham

Happy New Year was what I was expecting. I had completed making my 2002 goals, and I felt good about my farewell to 2001. As was my custom to the close out of one year and ushering in the possibilities of the new one, I wrote what I would like to accomplish in the next 365 days. I began the ritual by writing for a couple of days and then I set it aside for a day of spiritual guidance. I, in essence, tried to allow God to speak to the very desires of my heart.

With six categories outlined, I had the plan for my near future. I typed it up and placed it in my Day-Timer for easy access as a reminder of what I was working toward. I placed at the top of my list spiritual growth. *That's a nice path to seek,* I thought. I then followed it with personal health, finances, temperament, business plan and other. I purposefully and deliberately made subpointers of how I would ultimately carry out my development in this year.

With all this planning, I still had daily tasks requiring my attention. I had postponed some necessary house cleaning because I knew that I would have a long weekend. It was the Saturday before the Martin Luther King, Jr., holiday. I decided to give my immediate energy to the tidiness of my kitchen. It is a small box that you can count ten squares back then five across, keeping in mind to dodge the appliances, which protrude just enough to make me move around like a pinball in an arcade game.

I had pulled the trash, cleaned the refrigerator and tossed all the wilted and unwanted items that passed their expiration date. My son, Quincy, sat in the living room commemorating another Saturday with the *Fox Kids* line-up as Jewel, our cocker spaniel lay next to him.

Quincy is a sweet and very energetic six-year-old who has neither his father nor my personality. He is extremely gregarious, almost to a fault, and finds humor and enjoyment with loud noises, animation and stunts galore. He was in his Saturday trance, breathing and hypnotized with sheer entertainment.

I began to rinse and load the dishes in the dishwasher, which was Quincy's major annoyance. The thrust of the warm water gushed into his cartoon haze and interrupted his boy-made surround-sound system. He did as he always does—he turned the volume up to drown out my bleach, soap and water cocktail. I peeked over the shutter bar divider leading into the living room to see Quincy seated on the floor, wrapped in a quilt hand-sewn by my grandmother. He didn't seem to notice anything around him, not even the loud ring of the telephone.

I wanted him to answer it, but I knew that would be too much to ask for him to separate from his conjoined exchange of *Ninja Turtles* saving the city. I dried my hands and said, "Hello." There was a delay, so I repeated my greeting with more volume and a deeper tone. I heard a fuzzy yet very familiar "Hello …" The voice was distinct and surprising altogether. It jolted an instant emotion of anger in me that made the next words come out cold and uninviting.

"What do you want, Julius?"

"I've been trying to get in touch with you for years," he said.

The only reply I could generate was "Um-huh" with the tone that really conveyed "What the hell do you want?"

He cleared his throat and continued the conversation like he didn't receive any of my negative energy.

He told me that he didn't have much time, and he had someone do him a favor by calling me on three-way. The only thing that we agreed and were on one accord about was it had been a long time—seven years to be exact. I must have been mesmerized because I didn't remember much of the ten-minute conversation. What I do remember is my mouth said, "yes" before my mind's quick wit shot down his inquisition. I had agreed to allow him to write me and explain what he had been doing after our abrupt separation.

I disconnected the call, not knowing whether I wanted to get his letter or just hold on to wishing that he would forget me. I knew the removal from his remembrance was not an option, only because occasionally throughout the years, I would have sporadic voicemail messages indicating a request for me to return a call regarding Julius. Less than a year ago, I had a message from a chaplain asking me to call Cayuga Correctional Facility. I erased the invitation along with the contact information and rejected trying to make that connection again.

Julius' phone call altered all my plans to clean for that Saturday afternoon. Just hearing his voice induced me back in time and then switched gears to forward thoughts of what he might have to say. Julius' voice had stirred those stifled, buried and unsettled feelings that sent me into a haze much like Quincy's.

I sat in my dining room rewinding the video of my mind and stopped on February 1994. I was twenty-six, single and loving every moment of it. I had recently emancipated myself from a relationship that had more emotional distance than the 140 physical miles that separated us. More than four months earlier, I had ended a three-year tango of pretending that I was Corey's only dance partner.

Corey was twenty-nine, deep dark chocolate and a dreamer. He came off as being sensitive, caring and family-oriented, but what he was instead was reserved, quiet and uncomplimentary. Corey and I were good together as long as I phoned ahead and visited town sparingly. He tried to make me feel special by having me come by his job to pick up the key to his apartment, which was where I would relax and anticipate his kick-off of the weekend with me.

As I began to pull up old memories, I went further back in time trying to piece all of the past together. It was an October weekend and a lover's holiday, Sweetest Day 1993. I was going to enjoy how sweet Corey was going to be to me. I intended to have lunch with my brother's wife, Simone, who was a mover and a shaker—very driven and focused on her career. Her drive led her to cancel our lunch date, which left me with idle time to nap and watch soap operas at Corey's house.

I was lounging on the sofa, watching Erica Kane continue her diva life on *All My Children,* when I heard the tumbler of the door click. I didn't rush to get up because I assumed that Corey had taken a lunch break, and I was going to be his Ms. Goodbar. I rolled to my feet, only to turn and find this short, dark-skinned young woman entering the apartment with CDs and a stereo in hand. My face looked like I was clueless as to what I was observing. I probably even turned my head to the Scooby Doo sound bite of "I don't know." Her look reflected my feelings exactly. She entered fully into the living room, and we introduced ourselves.

She said with such manners, although probably not meaning it, "Pleased to meet you, Naomi."

I said, "Likewise, Lynne," knowing I didn't mean it. Lynne had been nicely servicing my boyfriend. I had suspected the presence of another woman, only because Corey's home furnishings increased probably more than his income had. He began wearing very nice jogging and walking suits, and he had the latest release of any R&B artist. It was uncharacteristic of him. He was never a slob in his appearance, but he also never rewarded himself with the current items I had been noticing.

After spending about an hour disclosing the last several months and realizing we were women living in parallel universes, I did what any self-respecting woman would do. I sprayed perfume on his sofa, grabbed my items and left. I had no intention of confronting him, only because that would indicate that I cared too much. I wanted to see if he would come clean.

I went to my brother's house and vented the day's experience to Simone. She laughed as I told her that I exited the apartment and the only sign remaining of me was my favorite fragrance. He would never again experience that delightful scent as he rolled over to nestle his head into my shoulder.

Corey called my brother's house that evening and tried to question me on how much I knew. I played along, hoping that Lynne had not told him of our meeting. I guess my presence was much too much for her to keep her mouth closed, which was very much like what she had been doing with her pocketbook. He and I verbally sparred; going back and forth with shouts and accusations, and I told him he never had to call me again.

Four months later, in the cold city of Cleveland, a hot little adult pajama party was bumping. I was bartending and archiving the scenes in the room. My job was to serve Royal Crown, Seven and Seven, Slow Gin Fizz and whatever the crowd asked for. It didn't matter that the only experience I had as a bartender was being the hand on the receiving end of a shot of 151. I liked my liquor dark, sweet and smooth, just like I wanted my men.

Joining me at the bar was my counterpart. He was medium brown and nice to look at, but not my type. However, as with most young adult parties, the women outnumbered the men, and he was in demand for more than his mixology skills. He would often leave the bar to dance with some lovely young lady who was half-dressed in skimpy lingerie and shoes that were made to make her feel like a supermodel.

I danced to the beat from behind the bar and enjoyed as much conversation with the men trying to lure me from my call to duty. I dressed more for fun than to excite. My attire was almost kiddylike compared to some of the baby-doll nighties that were sashaying around the room. I had on some spandex black men's briefs with checkered black-and-white men's boxer shorts on top. I accented it with a red pajama top that had a black poodle design on the front. I was cute, but by no means was I causing men to drool over me as if they were in heat. The red top complemented my sandy-brown hair and freckles.

I had turned several guys down to dance, but the deejay decided to slow it down, and my 151 buzz was kicking in. I noticed a tall, slender, dark brown guy watch my every move. He was too far away for me to get a good look at him, but his profile indicated that he was more than likely handsome because of his keen features. He observed me like he was reading a label that said, "She just might …" He glided over and asked my name. I initially thought I would make up a club name, but he was too attractive to just dismiss. I honestly replied, "Naomi."

He said, "You are one fine red bone, Naomi. I'm Julius. Would you like to dance?"

Dressed in cotton plaid skidz and a white wife-beater, he seemed to match my *I Love Lucy* sleepwear. I responded by following him to the dance floor. We danced, and he felt so good. We swayed to the begging sounds of Keith Sweat, but we didn't care because we were into the moment. I liked them tall, and I liked then strong, and more importantly I just liked him.

We talked very little because it was so congested and noisy. I liked him enough to give him my phone number. I had enjoyed meeting him, but I was committed to keeping my freedom. I had departed the distance relationship and wanted to keep as much emotional distance as possible while making the physical space almost disappear.

Julius called the following week, and I declined to return his call. I had other gentlemen callers who were eager to do some closing of that physical space more quickly than I was. He continued to call every three days. By the time we had gotten to the fourth repetition, I rewarded his diligence. We chatted briefly and made plans to get together in a couple of days.

We met at one of my favorite spots to enjoy someone's company, the 72nd Marina pier of Lake Erie. It was a great place to talk and get to know him. You can walk among the rocks and smell the Walleye along with the discarded beer bottles and refreshments that the fishermen would leave.

He and I had an instant connection, although I would not have conceded to it at the time. For our second date, we agreed to go see *Sugar Hill*, starring Wesley Snipes. I remember the movie and not much else about the time spent in the cinema. We returned to his sister, Dana's home on the west side of town. We pretended to watch a late-night talk show for a little while. At this time, I had no liquor in me, and the only desire I had was to feel Julius' flesh against mine. I shamelessly gave myself as I took him on the living room floor. It was a kismet experience, and everything felt so good.

We continued to spend time together. My intentions were to keep it at a pleasure level of simply a physical and sexual relationship. I wanted to enjoy Julius and for him to enjoy me—nothing more. We continued that consistently several times a week. I had experienced a significant amount of change in my life in a short time. I had just quit my job and was working on my own business, offering wedding consulting and desktop publishing services. We had afternoons together, early mornings and late nights, which led to later nights. While sex was very much our daily routine, we had begun to just have fun together. We would sit and talk for hours. I had filled most of my time with Julius. I was not growing my business nor was I motivated to do so. He had pacified me in such a way that I felt it had become unhealthy. My plan was not to throw my life into a man, especially one not working a daily job.

He had left town on a couple of occasions to go on the road with his father. From what Julius had shared with me during our afternoon chat sessions or early-morning pillow talk, his father owned his own trucking company. He would go on the road for a week or two at time, loading and unloading trucks. It seemed like a wonderful fit for my life, initially.

His schedule allowed me to concentrate on other things, like my livelihood, while he was out of town.

By late spring, I had spent well into my savings and had less income than my present spending and life could afford. I worked through a temporary agency, which fit my taste at the time. It helped subsidize my expenses and kept me close to the lifestyle to which I was accustomed.

When Julius would return from his travels with his father, we would hook up and resume seeing each other as if no time had passed. I had grown very use to his companionship and became increasingly aware that his trips were lengthening in time apart. We weren't a couple—or at least neither of us had admitted otherwise. The weather was heating up, and our relationship was too. I could see him as more than my companion, but I didn't understand his need to travel so frequently. Of course during the summer months, more people relocated, so he was on the road almost as much as off.

When we were together, you couldn't have convinced me that I wasn't the center of his attention. But when work called, there was no telling what he was doing. And I was destined not to repeat a long-distance relationship where another woman was living my corresponding life.

By late autumn, I had not increased my company's revenue or clientele. I was out of savings and needed to get a job. I had no strings attached or nothing keeping me grounded to my hometown. At that time, an old work acquaintance called and offered me a position in the capital city. I agreed because she sold me on the premise that "nothing is really keeping you there."

I planned my move, like a prideful father plans his pregnant daughter's shotgun wedding. I knew I had to pack and move. Thankfully, my brother had said I could stay with him and his family for a short time. I hadn't thought about affording the move or soliciting volunteers to assist in my relocation. I planned to make a clean break from my life. I told my frequent companion Julius of my poorly thought-out plan and departure.

Much to my surprise, he offered to get a friend and help me move. In my haste of uprooting, I did not give much attention or conversation to his offer. I accepted, and within two weeks, I was on my way to my new life. I began work at my new position at the beginning of October 1994. I stayed with my brother, Alex, for a couple of months while I searched for an apartment. I found a great townhouse with two bedrooms and gorgeous hardwood floors that I loved.

Julius had been to visit me a couple of times, and we were still very much enjoying each other's presence as well as bodies. He was still on the road repeatedly and seemed to love that life. We saw each other even less. By December, my place was ready for me to move in. Julius assembled his friend Malik, and I solicited my favorite cousin Myeisha's help. In the cold of winter, we were to load the seventeen-foot truck on Friday evening and drive from Cleveland to Columbus early Saturday morning.

The guys did a wonderful job and left single, lightweight boxes for Myeisha and me to put both in the truck and car. We made it to my new destination without any hiccups. Julius and I were to spend a week together after our two helpers returned to Cleveland. We all had such a good time together. Myeisha was feeling sportive and decided to hook up with Julius' friend Malik. They were a very unlikely couple, but sex can make two people kick desire aside in the name of lust and availability. Julius and I hardly noticed because we had our activities in play; and spent time almost exclusively together.

On Sunday night, Myeisha and Malik went on their two-hour journey home, leaving Julius and me time alone in a new place. We did what we had commonly done, spending hours in bed, and we spent even what was more surprising, intimate conversation time together. I revealed my feelings for him, and he did likewise, but neither of us owned up to the fact that our kicking it was just us living a pretense. He did things for me that no man had ever done. He took care of my little needs. While I was at work during that week, he unpacked my new home and put things away—from my underwear to my glassware. I had witnessed his tenderness and caring, yet I still spoke no words that bore witness to my true feelings. I couldn't admit to him that I was in love with him because I could not admit it to myself.

"Mom, I'm hungry," Quincy called, breaking my trance from my past. That Saturday afternoon left me feeling spent—and it wasn't from cleaning my ten-by-five rectangle of a kitchen. Julius' phone call had opened a door that had been shut just by pure neglect and stubbornness. I had just given this man of my past a couple of hours, not realizing that my girlfriend Tia was coming by with her two children.

I told her of my call, and Tia smiled and said, "How do you feel?"

I said, speaking the truth, but not knowing what it meant, "I don't know."

I enjoyed the rest of that January Saturday playing with my son and Tia's two children. I recognized that I had things to do in the present, and there was no more time to continue looking back. Julius was absent from my thoughts for the remainder of that weekend after I told Tia of his call.

On Thursday, January 24, I received evidence of Julius' initial request. He wrote a direct five-page letter saying exactly what he wanted. He explained how he had tried to contact me over this seven-year sabbatical, hoping one day to have this very opportunity.

Julius also told me of his feelings and his uncertainty of what they meant. He left it open for friendship, and at that time in my life, that was all I was able to entertain. He gave me a brief overview of his plans and where his head and heart were. I connected with him in the very first letter, but I slowed it down for a couple of weeks.

I finally responded to Julius' letter and his next one arrived exactly four days after I mailed mine. I was hard on him. The walls went up, but the words still kept coming out on paper. He wrote religiously. It was like he knew once he caught my attention, he could crack the shell enough to be truly heard.

I could not match the pace of Julius' letters, nor did I want to. In the first three months, it seemed like he wrote me at least three times a week. He talked about plans and what had gone on in his life. Julius stayed focused on his feelings for me, and I pushed and pushed to squash that noise. I wasn't feeling going back. We had had our time and chance in life. In my mind that had come and certainly gone and was never to be repeated.

I did enjoy his company once again, and I was unsure why. I found myself protesting his advances at every turn, and I was committed to being a friend as long as that was all he wanted. I wrote to encourage him, to entertain me and in response to his questions, often asking questions of my own.

By March, we had kept the post office in business single-handedly—or at least that was how it felt. Letters would cross in the mail, and it was nothing to have more than a dollar of postage on a single correspondence. He kept me company and busy, and I'm sure I did the same for him.

What was very similar and familiar to me was that I kept it real with him on most levels. When we first met, that was my motto. My emancipation then almost mirrored my current one. Before, I explored my freedom of our sexuality; this time I explored the freedom of my emotional and spiritual being. We communicated for months without ever hearing each other's voices.

Because I typically evaluate my goals quarterly, I pulled out that New Year's list and revisited my directed path. I recounted my spiritual growth of regular church attendance, Sunday school for Quincy, daily quiet time, reading my bible and a small women's bible study. I had found some success with that goal. Because I had been trying to evangelize Julius, I was reading God's word and praying like I had not done in quite some time.

I had daily communion with God in my prayers on my way to work. I asked myself what was I doing with Julius, and I prayed that I was not leading him on. He consistently expressed his feelings for me, and I spent much energy denying and rebutting it. He stayed his course and worked his plan. Julius was committed to what he wanted, and over time we continued to really talk about everything. He eventually shared with me his reason for his incarceration. Julius gave limited information leading up to it, but spoke freely of his steadfast feelings for me. I was flattered, but I still viewed this relationship as a rearview mirror one, in which he was just an opportunity of the past gone by.

By April, my goals had been evaluated, and I concluded that nowhere was there a plan for friendships or relationships. It was about me becoming what I saw as a better person. I knew that I had developed feelings for Julius that I did not want to resurrect. I decided to focus on my initial number one goal, so I turned my desires to God—the ultimate relationship.

On April 24, I wrote a letter to God asking for my soul mate. I wrote forty things that I wanted in a mate. I folded the half-sized bright fuchsia paper in thirds and placed it in my bible. Those three pages were my honest request to God for my mate.

Lists have a funny way of bringing you back to what you really want to focus on. My letter to God was not for God to check off what He had for me, but for me to remain focused on what I considered important. I was building an expectation that I knew was not impossible but highly improbable at that time.

Julius continued to write, and we had plans for me to visit him in June, which was a good month for me for a couple of reasons. Quincy would spend part of the summer with his father, Corey, which left time for me to travel. It was also my birthday month, and I very much love birthdays. I use that time to celebrate the gift of life, which is the most valuable lesson I got from my father's early death. I make special plans, even if it happens to be a festive dinner alone.

The first Saturday in June was the date for Julius and me to see each other again. Two weeks before I was to travel to Collins Correctional Facility to visit him, he was relocated to another facility seventy miles away. He asked if I wanted to cancel the trip. I think Julius sensed my nervousness and apprehension for this reunion. If actions don't speak louder than words, then I may have just screamed that I was feeling something for him other than friendship. The fact that my desire had grown far beyond my fear was the first concrete indication that I was living a life in denial. My decision to make a trip almost four hundred miles away alone and on highways I had never driven revealed that I was hiding behind clever words.

I packed up my son's clothing for several weeks with his father and a weekend bag for myself. The Friday afternoon I was to leave, a long letter from Julius arrived in the mail, but since my schedule was tight, his conversation with me had to wait until I was in the privacy of my hotel room.

I arrived in the small town of Hornell, which was almost twenty miles away from Julius' facility. Livingston was the very first correctional facility that I'd entered. On Saturday morning, I got schooled on the forms to complete, the wait to get shuffled from one room to another and the incredible nervousness of what the unknown was bringing. I met kind people that day who spoke to me and told me the ins and outs of entering a New York correctional facility.

The very first gentleman I met in the visiting center was a minister visiting an inmate to encourage and pray with him. He explained that I had gotten processed faster than anyone he had witnessed. He shared with me that he was originally from Cincinnati, Ohio. In my nervousness, I never shared any information about myself. He walked with me, leading the way through all the buzzes and clicks of the metal releasing and closing back as we entered the prison. After clearing the metal detectors, getting my hand stamped with UV black light ink, being assigned a place to sit and watching all the exchanges of greetings between inmates and their visitors, I fought back my overwhelming feeling to stand up and leave.

As I sat and waited for Julius to walk through the door in the front of the room, I saw sons greet their mothers, daughters, wives and girlfriends. There were very few men in the visiting room that day, other than those being held against their will or the ones being paid to hold them captive. I observed the rush to vending machines and all the hustle and bustle of getting settled. The visitors shopped from these machines like Thanksgiving hostesses browse the grocery store aisles looking for the perfect ingredients for their masterpiece dinners. I have come to understand the ceremony and importance of eating together on those visits, but at the time it seemed very strange to me.

In this communal visiting room with playing card–sized tables, each with four chairs, I noticed a poster on the wall that read BUT FOR THE GRACE OF GOD, GO I. A sense of peace came over me as I awaited the face of my long-missed friend. Julius walked through the door, looking very much the same. His hair was cornrowed to the back and had been freshly braided. He had on a tan shirt and state-issued greens. He walked to the officer's station and handed him something. The officer told Julius the letter and number that corresponded to the table where I was seated. I later found out that Julius had handed the officer his inmate ID before walking toward me. He was nervous and trying to hide his excitement. He gently smiled, and I stood to greet him with a platonic hug. When I felt his hand touch the small of my back, I yielded my body to his, telling him that I was happy to see him as well. My delight was in part relief that I had made it to my destination safely. I was able to see on the surface that other than the aging around his eyes, prison had not destroyed Julius' mental being. I was not completely comfortable in his presence. I could tell the way he looked at me that friendship was not what he was willing to settle for.

We talked and I, too, bought food for us from those vending machines. Julius and I shared our first meal together in more than seven years. We talked about our children, families and goals and reminisced of the past fun we'd shared. I held the thought in my mind, *I can't go back,* but my heart was attempting to drown out the reminder of this motto. We took a few pictures together. Julius looked so relaxed in the photos, his normal confidence was shining through, but my poses were less a complement to his. I revealed my unease and perhaps uncertainty.

My desire continued to drive the fear away. At the end of our visit, I embraced him good-bye and told him that I didn't know when or if I would make it back to see him. Julius thanked me for my company, and his sadness at my departure saddened me also. He had planned for my visit carefully and was certain to make sure that I had something to take home telling me how thankful he was that I'd visited with him. He wrote me a letter and had a birthday card made for me. It is one of the most beautiful cards I have ever received. Julius' tenderness, kindness and thoughtfulness became a reminder of the person I once knew. I connected with him on that day on a level even more profound than was in our past.

I returned home, and we continued to write each other. My feelings had changed, and he became more demanding of my time. I understood it, but I also rebelled against it. Both of us recognized that the summer had created something new. It kicked the door off the hinges, and I could no longer just turn away. However, going forward was a reminder that he came with hurdles and some pretty heavy baggage. I stifled my feelings constantly by reprising the same old words, "Don't go back. There is no future in reverse." As much as I practiced those words in my mind, my feelings were growing and moving steadily in Julius' direction.

By September, I had visited Julius two more times and requested for the block to be removed from my phone. We now had immediate responses to each other, unlike what the letters had been providing. There is a different connection with someone in spoken verse, and our friendship blossomed all the more.

By the time autumn arrived, school was back in session for Quincy, and my life as mother and provider took their rightful place. I was the PTA president, manager of the fastest growing division in my company, serving in the community and volunteering continuously. My body was getting weary, my emotions were indistinguishable, and Julius continued to be my number one supporter from afar. Our relationship had changed in what seemed like a twinkling of an eye.

Julius had used the time of our letter writing to tune into my needs, and he even retreated in his advances. I valued his friendship, but I was still not convinced of the direction of which I had been following.

There were times when my letter writing came to a snail's pace because I felt that I was still leading him on. We would talk about how I felt, and usually he was the best at listening. Julius had come to a place that if I chose him, he would get his ultimate prize, but if I didn't, he would still value our friendship. I had no pressure from him, but I self-imposed my own.

I was wrestling with what to do with Julius, and he was at peace with where we were. I continued to write, and he did too. By winter, we both knew that there would be no visits. Western New York's weather can be treacherous and unpredictable. It made my desire to see him increase, and I longed for his presence. I matched that passion with intensified letter writing, and he responded equally and accordingly.

We had been faithfully communicating for more than a year. Julius and I had creative ways to celebrate his birthday and Thanksgiving, and he even honored my enthusiasm for Christmas. He was my closest friend. He had confided in me, and I likewise opened myself up to some of the most painful and vulnerable experiences of my life. At first, those intimate moments came cautiously and very sparingly. Julius had disclosed everything leading up to his crime and how he had arrived on such a devastating doorstep, and I cherished him even more. He expressed how the loss of his father while incarcerated had affected him, and I shared the similarities in losing my father as a child.

During those cold months, his tenderness eased my mind and comforted my spirit. I still had not come to a place of clarity for our direction. I would at times become quarrelsome, hoping that he would decide that I was too much work for him. I threw curve balls, either through lack of writing or emotional withdrawal. Julius seemed to be able to match ambivalence with self-assurance and reassurance.

By March, I had early spring fever. I was ready to visit Julius, and he had relocated to a closer facility. I was now anxious to see him, not anxious about seeing him. I had changed. I had come to some level of balancing my uncertainty and reservation with treasuring who Julius is and what our friendship meant to me. It was as I saw it selfish, but I was giving him the best that I was at that time, and he was likewise.

Before the weather broke, I was en route to the new facility and the open arms of his embrace. I was now on my way to being a veteran to the similarities of each New York facility. As with most things, experience brings about comfort. I visited him once a month for the next few months because June would arrive and bring about the freedom and availability to travel.

I was now one of the many women in the visiting room who had my quarter routine, vending-machine run and appropriate prison attire, which covered almost every portion of skin, down to a science. I would even make a game out of how long it was from the time I arrived at the facility until I saw Julius' face. We had come to a place where we created normalcy in our relationship. What started as a platonic embrace led to a kiss on the cheek then became a woman standing up to passionately kiss for the brief time it was allowed. I had not allowed Julius to claim me as his girlfriend, woman or any of those other labels that indicated a more personal relationship. Yet, my actions were screaming volumes above what my words would say.

Over the months, I had forced my holiday and birthday enthusiasm onto Julius. I am still not sure if he really felt it or just went along with all my celebrations for my sake, but he was looking forward to our June visit. It was very similar to the others, but I had a birthday coming. I had plans to visit Put-in-Bay my birthday, so our visit was again that first weekend in June. I drove I-90 East, enjoying the warmth of the season. I was on my way to see my best friend. Julius held secrets and events in confidence, and I loved him for that.

I arrived at the facility before 10:00 A.M., as usual, with the hopes of seeing Julius before 11:30. I was very anxious, and the visit seemed different from the many others. I entered the facility and took my assigned seat, just as trained. We were past the eleven o'clock hour, so I knew the count would further delay Julius' arrival. I sat at the table, as I had done before and watched men hugging their mothers, daughters, wives and girlfriends, and I got very sad. The melancholy took over my emotions, and I couldn't understand what had troubled me so. I lost myself in a room full of people because I now had become one of them. I was in tune with what a relationship with an inmate meant. Up until that June visit, it was casual for me, or that's how I perceived it. I realized that day that I really loved my companion, my friend—my best friend. I felt trapped and repulsed. Julius was expected to arrive at my table in hopefully less than thirty minutes when I felt the tears in my eyes. I was at a point where going back was the exact place that I was sitting. I went to the restroom to wipe my face and remove any visible evidence of my sorrow. I stood in the mirror, and the tears began to flow. I didn't know how to pull myself together, but I knew I had to. I wiped away the tears and tried to mask all my oceans of emotions. I returned to my seat and practiced my quick and light smile, which I usually shared with other female visitors once our gazes met.

On that day, Julius made it to the visiting room right before noon, which meant we would only have three hours of conversation. God must have known that I could not fake it or entertain Julius that long without revealing all the things that I had been feeling. Julius came through the door in the front of the room, and he looked more handsome than ever. He had a fresh haircut and a lovely Muslim oil scent that imitated any expensive men's store designer fragrance. He was so happy to see me that I don't think he recognized my sadness. He immediately sat down and began talking about how happy he was. His enthusiasm when I visited reminded me of a kid when he shows his mother a good report card.

As we settled into the meat of our visit, he asked, "What's wrong?"

I said, "Nothing" and changed the subject to discuss my birthday plans.

I should have been given an Academy Award for my performance because he continued with our visit very much as normal. I was able to enjoy his company, which came as no surprise, and Julius' personality made it easy. I don't remember any special significance in our conversation that day, but I knew that I was going to have to come to grips with our relationship. I could no longer brush it away as us being just friends. I was having a personal war with the relationship and this man being incarcerated.

On the drive home, I turned off the radio. If someone had been joining me on my travels they would have observed complete silence although the noise in my brain was deafening. I managed to make it home safely, and I tried to put those thoughts out of my mind. Sunday morning I awoke early with Julius heavy on my mind and heart. I decided to go to my coping mechanism and make a list of fears and reservations on the left and advantages and desires on the right. At first, the left side was stockpiling item after item. I included the major and obvious like Julius being incarcerated. I also included the less prominent, like his lack of income and the distance. The list continued, with the left pulling ahead. I even included an intangible, like "I can't go back." I did attempt to balance the list with how Julius made me feel, his kindness and tenderness. I didn't revisit any previous items; I just kept the tally flowing. After spending an immeasurable amount of time, I laid the list down and went to prepare for church.

I went to church that day and felt freed because for the first time I had at least admitted that I was afraid and why. I have always heard the first step to recovery is to admit you have a problem. I was one better because I had identified what the problem was. I was well on my way to recovery. I returned from church, renewed and refreshed. I changed my clothes and made lunch. I sat down at the table, and right next to me was that list from my early-morning enlightenment. I glanced over it, circled one item and placed it aside again. While I was on my way to recovery, I was also sure that I was not going to let my problem stand in the way of enjoying the day. I placed my dishes in the sink and went on my merry way. I visited with friends and family that Sunday afternoon, and I gained some peace and perspective too.

The next Saturday, Julius called me. I answered to hear, "You have a call from an inmate at a New York correctional facility ..." I pressed three, which would connect me to my friend almost instantaneously.

He said, "Hello, sweetness." He continued to talk and ask how my day was going. Something soothing in his voice quieted me in my spirit. I allowed him to update me on how his week had gone. He continued to talk, and I intervened with "I love you." It was such a meek, quiet tone that it made his response ironic.

He stopped dead in the middle of his sentence like a train wreck had occurred, and said, "What did you say?"

I hesitated as I read the circled item on the paper from my previous week's list. I said, "Hmm. I love you," with more boldness like he had already heard this before. It quieted him, almost to the point of awkward silence. I heard the slightest sniffle, and I said, "Did I make you cry?"

Julius did not answer my question directly, but he said, "I have waited so long for this, and it sounds so good." He was almost whispering, which was bringing the tone of the conversation back to where I had started. When I released what had been held so deeply and preciously in my heart, it was as if angels were rejoicing in my truth. It was magical, special, and I found solace in that moment. My desire was greater than my fear. In the course of a few minutes, I had arrived at a moment where I was no longer dreading looking back or what I had labeled going back. And in my resolve to face that fear, I found that I was not going backward at all. I was stepping into my heart's reversal of fortune, and I was the one who was the biggest benefactor of this truth. I smiled and embraced the thought, *List have a funny way of bringing you back.*

--- ❀ ---

"I am just thankful that God found me deserving enough

To present such a precious gift as your love …

But I am even more thankful

That I was smart enough to grab hold and never let go."

—*Author Unknown*

Each time I read this quote I am reminded of the day that Terry and I met so many years ago. Our life together, yes behind the wall, has truly been abundant. There have been ups and downs but most importantly, there has always been love.

This is the story of Terry and Rayna—a tribute to our love at first sight.

—*Rayna*

How Do I Love Thee? Him, Us and Me

Rhonda L. Harris

"Ain't no such thing as love at first sight." I have said those words more times than I can count to my girlfriends and cousins whenever we talk about men, but the moment I saw him, our eyes met and I knew he was "the one." There was some invisible force pushing me, nudging me in his direction. I had never felt anything like it. What was it? What should I do? How could I act on it? There I was in the photo room to take pictures with another man, another inmate. How could I now turn to the one I was visiting and say, "Guess what? I want him." I would have started an all-out war behind those walls, so I restrained myself and said nothing.

Terry is his name. Um, Terry, the Latin translation for smooth and polished. Oh yeah, his birth name was most fitting. He hadn't even said a word to me, but I knew … I just knew. Terry was one of the photographers taking pictures that day. When our eyes met, he was sitting at a desk filling out debit slips for the guys so their inmate accounts could be deducted for the costs of the pictures.

Terry and Shawn, the guy I was visiting that day, exchanged the customary "what's up" to each other. I'll tell you more about Shawn in a minute. While I was busy posing with Shawn, all I kept thinking about was a way to make him leave the photo room first so I could talk to Terry. I didn't know what I would say but I knew that I had to say something. I have never been the pursuer—I'm always the one being pursued—but something inside of me simply said jump. When Shawn and I were done taking pictures, I told him I would be a few minutes getting back to the visiting room because I was going to the restroom. I thought this was my chance. Shawn walked out of the photo room, and I walked toward the desk where Terry was sitting. Before I could say anything, Terry touched my hand, and there was magic. He handed me a folded piece of paper. I unfolded it to read TERRY WILLIAMS 83AH555. He said, "Please write me." I screamed inside, *Oh my God. He can read my mind. He must be the one.*

Was this fate? I looked up from the note to say, "Nice to meet you, Terry. I'm Rayna." I was so nervous. Terry sat at that desk looking so good. He seemed nervous and confident all at the same time. I'm sure he was a little nervous trying to scoop up someone else's girl in a prison, even though I was not Shawn's girl at all. I didn't know what to say next so I started to walk away. He said, "Rayna, you don't have a last name?" I gave him the biggest smile I could and said, "Of course I do. You'll never forget my last name because it's the same as yours." I grinned from ear to ear. He replied with a smile just as big as mine. I was flirting, y'all, just being so fast. I gave him a wink, and I walked away. Even though I knew nothing about this man other than his name and DIN (designated inmate number), I knew that he was special. It felt like something special was brewing. Was it our destiny to be one? He read my mind. We had the same last name. This had to be fate. What we would both later learn is that our meeting was God's blessing to us both.

I felt like I was in heaven and hell at that very moment. I was sitting at the table with this sorry excuse for a man daydreaming about "the man." I couldn't wait for visiting hours to be over. It was the last time I was coming to see Shawn. I don't know what my cousin Kim was thinking when she suggested that I write him. He seemed nice, but he also seemed a little sneaky, like he had something to hide. What I disliked most about Shawn was that he was just so clueless about everything that really mattered. All I kept doing for the rest of the visit was wishing for the day to quickly come to an end.

On the long bus ride home, all I did was replay over and over the few precious moments that Terry and I shared. I couldn't help it. I kept gazing at the piece of paper he had given me. His handwriting was so neat, especially for a man. Terry is one fine specimen. He has caramel skin, dark brown eyes that just seem to sparkle so brightly when he smiled—perfect pearly whites that just gleam—and black naturally curly hair. I wished I'd had the nerve to run my fingers through his curls. I wondered if the hair on his chest was just as curly as the hair on his head. I even wondered about the hair down there. The aromatic woodsy scent of his cologne was like a magnet drawing me in. I wondered how tall he was. I couldn't really tell from the way he was sitting, but he seemed to be of average height—about five-eight or five-nine. He just looked good, even in his state greens. I knew that a man who could look that good in a state prison uniform could sure hang the hell out of a suit. As I drifted off to sleep, I had visions of Terry in an Armani suit.

I got home around 1:00 A.M. Thank God for mothers. My mom spent the weekend at my house caring for my babies. I was just too excited to sleep. I wanted to wake her and tell her that I had found the one, but I was not ready to play Twenty Questions with her all night long.

It was time though to pull out my favorite stationery and write my first letter to Terry. Since we literally knew nothing about each other other than our names, what would I say? How much would I tell him? I decided to do the opposite of what I did when I wrote Shawn for the first time—tell the truth. I didn't really lie to Shawn in my first letter. I just told him all of the wonderful things about myself, and I neglected all of the not-so-wonderful things. This time was going to be different. I was going to give Terry the ultimate snapshot of me, so I began to write. Letter number one was really a pure image of me. I shared with Terry most of my loving qualities and delicately shared some of my traits that are not so loving like the fact that I'm an only child and I'm accustomed to getting my way ninety-nine percent of the time, and when I don't, there is usually hell to pay. I figured that I gave him enough to pique his interest or run him away, but not enough for him to think that he had me all figured out. I finished my ten-page letter at 5:00 A.M., an hour before I had to get up and ready myself for work. I hadn't even realized how much time had gone by since I started writing. Mondays were always hellish days for me at the bank. The check clearing operation that I managed was truly the last place most bankers wanted to be. My department was plagued by early mornings and mandatory overtime so I never knew when I was going home. No one went home until the work was done. So there I was going to run this unit on one hour of sleep. Infatuation will make you do some crazy things. I turned off the lights and slept like a baby for all of sixty minutes.

I woke up refreshed and exhausted. I knew this was going to be a long day. I turned on the coffee pot, woke up my babies and went about our day. I was a newly divorced single mother. My babies were two and four years when Terry and I met. Trina, my oldest, is truly her father's child, in every sense of the word. Jada, my baby, is the mirror image of me, only many shades lighter, but our mannerisms and features are almost identical.

My children are my life. Their dad and I married much too young—I was twenty-one and he was nineteen. We got married only because we were pregnant with Trina, not because we were in love. Yes, I loved him, but he was not ready for this commitment. He had not learned how to take care of himself let alone a wife and a baby. The short version of a long, ugly story is that Darnell assumed that adultery, not monogamy, was a requirement for marriage. I tried to be the martyr and live the "let's stay together for the kids" fairytale, until I couldn't take his emotional abuse any longer. I simply woke up one morning and said to myself that it was the day of a new beginning and packed all of his shit, which wasn't much because all he had when he moved in was literally the clothes on his back. I went to the hardware store, bought new locks and installed them myself. I put all of his belongings on the back deck and taped a note to the door that read, LOVE DON'T LIVE HERE ANYMORE. YOUR STUFF IS ON THE DECK. IF YOU DON'T HAVE IT OUT OF HERE BY TRASH DAY, IT WILL BE SET OUT ON THE CURB. I filed for divorce three weeks later.

As our marriage was ending I had some new beginnings. I graduated from college and even started working on my master's degree. After the marriage ended, I decided that I was going to spend the rest of my parenting days focused on my children. I was determined to be a single working Supermom. I was going to be totally devoted to my kids, not letting any man or any semblance of a relationship interfere with my parenting. I decided that when the girls went off to college, some sixteen years later, then I would concentrate on finding a mate with whom to live happily ever after. Our Father who art in heaven had another plan.

As I nervously dropped Terry's letter in the mailbox, my mind began to work overtime. The psychologist in me began to analyze everything. I wondered if maybe I had given him too much information, maybe not enough. I began to speculate on what his responses would be. Of course I wanted to know what he did to land himself in prison. I wished that I knew how much time he had and how much time he had done. I asked myself all sorts of questions that I didn't have answers to. Would he think that my having two children was a bad thing. Did he even like kids? Would he think I was crazy because I told him I had never shacked with a man and never would? Would he react the same way the men out here in the free world do when I tell them that the next man with whom I share my body will be my husband? Would he think I was too cocky because I told him that I was an educated Black woman? I hoped he wouldn't think that I was an "inmate groupie" because I was visiting Shawn and I might potentially begin visiting him. What would his boys think about that and me? I had to shake those thoughts away, but just as I did, I began to question what the hell I was doing.

I am a well-educated sister with a great job, making good money so why was I even daydreaming about an inmate? I own my own condo, I drive a Volvo and I have six months' savings in the bank. Why was I so moved by this guy? Was I just lonely and reaching out to someone who reached out to me? What did I really think was going to come of this? What did Terry do to end up in prison? Was he ever coming home? How far would I be willing to go if things turned serious? *Enough,* I said to myself.

It was only 10:00 A.M. I was sleep deprived, and I had a headache that wouldn't quit. The phone on my desk wouldn't stop ringing. My processing projections for the day were so far off that I might have been the cause of the federal reserve bank overdrafting the next morning—something that is not tolerated by the management. I had to put Terry out of mind as much as I could until I received his response, and get back to work before I got fired.

Eleven days later I came home to find a thick envelope from Terry waiting for me in the mailbox. I had to get prepared to open it. My hands were shaking. I was laughing at everything and nothing all at the same time. I fixed dinner for the girls, and I gave them their baths, read them a story and then it was lights out. I had to go read Terry's letter. I felt like I was preparing for a date. I took a shower and moisturized my body with the same fragrance I wore the day Terry touched my hand. I put on one of my sexy nighties, climbed under the covers and opened my letter.

As I opened it, I could smell Terry. He laced it with his scent—the same one he wore the day we met. The first thing I read was a quote by Cyril Connolly: "Life is a maze in which we take the wrong turn before we have learnt to walk."

Y'all know that I was instantly impressed. Based on my brief "friendship" with Shawn, I had stereotyped inmates to be guys who didn't have command of the English language, were uneducated, couldn't speak proper English and damn sure couldn't write it, but Terry surprised me. Unlike me, Terry began his letter by jumping right in with the not-so-wonderful stuff. He told me about the maze of his life and how he took a wrong turn when he started selling drugs and then later began using them. Those same drugs were a prime factor in his committing murder.

My initial reactions were mixed. My feelings of awe for Terry were coupled with instant fear and panic. He was a convicted murderer. I felt like I had to stop whatever this was because there was no way that I could ever feel safe in the company of a murderer, and I sure as hell couldn't have my babies around one. I closed my eyes, took a deep breath and prayed for a clear heart and mind as I continued to read.

Terry then wrote about all of the things that he had learned since coming to prison some twelve years prior. He learned how to walk. He found Islam and believed that it saved his life. He felt that the belief and obedience to a higher power helped him rise above himself and was the driving force in changing him from the man he was when he entered prison into the man who was presenting himself before me then. Terry's admission that he was Muslim added another element of speculation into my heart and mind. How could I, a Christian woman, get seriously involved with a Muslim man? Who was his God? Who was Allah? Were our Gods the same? Were we unequally yoked? Did we not worship the same God just because he called him Allah and I called him Jesus? I continued to pray for clarity as I read.

Terry talked about his character and personality, describing himself as trustworthy, caring, understanding, loyal and God-fearing. I have to tell you that I was very impressed by what I read, not just because of what he said, but because of how he presented himself. This man could write. His words seemed to flow like poetry. It was obvious that he put a lot of time, energy, effort and thought into every chosen word. His intelligence was evident in every sentence that he formed. He was brilliant. He had to be educated. He was obviously well read to begin his letter with a quote from someone I hadn't even heard of—and I profess to know a little about almost everything.

I held on to my reservations, yet I was intrigued just the same. Terry told me that he loves kids. He said that he always had his little cousins hanging with him when he was in the street. More importantly though he said that kids loved him. I knew from that moment that my girls would be the litmus test to see if Terry's character was as true as his words—you know how kids and dogs just have that knack for detecting scum right off the bat?

My girlfriends and I use what we term the one-call test to determine if a guy is worth continuing conversing with. We don't believe in going on date after date only to find out after many wasted hours of our precious time that the guy is a jerk. One telephone conversation is all it takes to know whether he's worth spending anymore time on. So in my response to Terry, I gave him my phone number. I needed to hear him speak. For all I knew he got together with some of the fellas and wrote my letter as some group project to try to run game. I had to test the waters for myself. I mailed the letter and patiently waited for the day the phone would ring and I would hear, "You have a collect call ..."

In the meantime, while I was waiting to hear from Terry I began to dig a bit deeper into some spiritual study. I wanted to know more about Islam. Why did so many brothers convert to Islam once they went inside? What were the tenets that their faith relied on? I needed to get a better understanding of the religion as a whole. I went to the Bible to search for what it said about interfaith relationships. I needed to get down on my knees and pray for guidance in this situation. I have always been a firm believer that nothing in life occurs by accident, but to teach us or reveal something to us.

Everything that happens does so according to the will of God. What was Terry's introduction into my life here to teach me, show me? Were we destined to be great friends? Was Terry my destiny for more than friendship? Was he sent into my life to be the husband I wasn't sure I wanted and the father my babies needed? What did this all mean? I waited faithfully and prayerfully for answers.

It was a cold sunny Sunday afternoon the first time Terry called. The girls and I had gone to church that morning. We came home, and I had cooked dinner. The girls were in their playroom playing, and I was relaxing. The telephone rang, and I immediately heard, "You have a collect call …" My heart started racing. It was Terry. *Oh, God. Oh, God, this is it. Please, Lord, send me a sign,* I prayed. After accepting the charges, I said, "Hello," and the sexiest melodic voice I had ever heard said, "Hello, sweetheart. How are you?" I wanted to just scream. I could have died right there on the spot. I was happy and very suspicious too. I guess it was my nature to be suspicious and untrusting—yes, this is leftover baggage from my ex; but I held onto that phone and simply listened. I let Terry do most of the talking and boy could he talk. After exchanging the normal pleasantries, he talked about our introduction and how he had felt smitten every since. I commented on my feelings about the same. Those thirty minutes went way too fast. Despite my qualms, we had a great first conversation. Something inside of me again told me that he was the one. Our telephone time seemed to fly by so quickly, and neither of us wanted it to end. He called back two more times. From the first telephone conversation, I think we both knew that something greater than the both of us was at work. We ended our first of many Sunday telephone marathons saying that we'd write often and talk the following Sunday. We wrote numerous letters. Each one that arrived felt like a date with Terry. It was our time to connect just as couples out in the real world do on "real" dates. I would race home to the mailbox, anxious to see his beautiful handwriting on the outside of an envelope. Terry and I had three or four dates a week.

I found myself thinking about Terry all of the time. He had sent me some pictures of himself that I stared at every chance I got. I reread his letters over and over at night, as if they were the best book that I had ever read. I was really starting to fall for him. About two months into our writing and talking to each other, Terry asked me to come and see him. He said that he wanted to look into my eyes and really talk to me, that he needed to know if what he was starting to feel was real. Those words just seemed to melt my heart. He was so sincere. I hurried the week along so I could make that six-hour drive Friday night up to Plattsburgh to prepare for my first weekend with Terry. I knew that this week-end would mark the beginning of many that my mom would be called upon to do her grandmotherly duties of babysitting. I dropped the girls off to Granny and I hit the road. Our first visit was magical. When he walked into the visiting room, our eyes met, and it felt like love at first sight all over again. Of course it wasn't our first sighting but it was our first time seeing each other since our friendship had begun. He walked over to greet me with a nice hug, and he pulled out my chair for me to sit down. *I've got a real gentleman here,* I thought. While Terry and I sat there making eyes at each other, the word of my visit was making its way back to Shawn. I immediately asked Terry if this was going to be a problem for him inside. He assured me that everything would be fine. I heard the same voice again telling me that he was the one. We had such a great time. We talked and talked, laughed a lot and talked some more. We had the best conversations. We talked about our childhoods, how we grew up. Terry was raised in an average middle-class, two-parent household. He learned that I was raised by a single mother and that I am Cherokee Indian and Afri-can-American. Terry's father is a small-framed fair-skinned Cuban and his mother is a full-figure, dark-skinned African-American. It is kind of ironic but our physique somewhat echoes that of his parents, which was kind of cool, I thought. Terry is a few shades lighter than I am. He has an average build, but he is much shorter than I first thought—only five-six. I have mahogany skin and am definitely a full-figured woman.

We talked about our dreams for the future. Terry told me he wants to own his own business someday, helping inmates and their families with everything from legal issues to maintaining the foundations of their relationships. The heart of this man shone through in everything he said and did. I told Terry how I longed to be a professor and a published author. We talked and talked about what seemed like everything. We talked about so many things from sports, to politics, to money, racism and sexism. The time just flew by. It was 3:00 P.M. before we knew it, and visiting hours were coming to a close. As I pre-pared to leave, Terry helped me with my coat and kissed me on the cheek as we said good-bye.

Day two of our first weekend visit was much more of the same. We contin-ued to get to know each other by sharing our experiences. I was smitten, and I believe that Terry was too. We took our first pictures together that day. We looked so happy, like we were made for each other. The corrections officer who was in the photo room when we entered even mentioned that we were a cute couple. *Wow,* I thought, *a CO noticed us.* There had to be some aura surrounding us. Something enchanting was definitely happening between us.

How do I love thee? With every inch of my being I was falling in love with Terry. How could I fall in love with an inmate? Why would I fall in love with an inmate? What kind of life would we have? Would I be happy? Should I turn and run away? Should I stay?

I relied on my faith when I decided to stay. I heard only positive messages from The Father about Terry and our relationship. I never heard Him tell me to walk away, like He had when I met the girls' dad. With each passing day our thoughts became consumed with one another. The mailbox always seemed to be overflowing. I was spending some good money buying stationery and stamps so I could write Terry every day. Terry and I fell madly in love. We had decided that it was time for his test—the kids test.

I made the next weekend visit to see Terry with my babies. I have to tell you it was the ride from hell. This was the first road trip I had ever made with the girls. I did not know that Trina had motion sickness until it was too late. We had just passed Syracuse. I was driving sixty-five miles per hour when I heard the first gag. I didn't know what to do. I was driving on a freeway, and my baby was in the backseat upchucking. I pulled over immediately to the side of the road. She was okay, just covered in puke. Thankfully the next rest stop was just five miles away. As I parked, I began hearing the voice of doubt enter in, asking me, "What the hell are you doing? Is he worth all of this?"

Even though common sense probably would have dictated that I turn the car around and go back home, my heart told me that Terry was worth it, to be strong and do what I came to do. I had to clean both of the girls up. I basically had to bathe them with baby wipes and change their clothes. Next came the ordeal of cleaning out the backseat of the car. Ugh! Why does seeing vomit make you feel like you have to vomit? I guess it's the same thing as how seeing someone yawn makes you yawn. I purchased my first ever tube of Dramamine that day and have never been without it since. I was paranoid after that so much so that I gave Jada Dramamine too. She always asked me why she had to take it because she didn't throw up. I told her that same thing that all of our mothers have told us at one time or another: "Because I said so." We walked into the facility Saturday morning, and I was so nervous, more about the girls' first impressions of being inside of a prison than about them meeting Terry. I hoped and prayed they wouldn't be scared by the sounds of the clanging doors and seeing the bars all around. To my surprise, they were awesome. They got a kick out of the metal detectors. Trina's earrings made the detectors ring, so she had to walk through with her hands over her ears. She thought this was the coolest game she had ever played. The innocence of children is such a beautiful thing.

When we walked into the visiting room, their gazes immediately went to the play area. Cartoons were on the TV, and there were lots of toys just waiting for little hands to pick them up. Their first words were, "Mommy, can we go play?" I told them to wait a few moments until they met Terry and then they could go. They were on their best behavior, not because they were excited about meeting Terry, but because they knew that if they misbehaved I wouldn't let them go into the play area. Terry came into the room, and our eyes met. I watched his every step. He seemed to just glide across the room. I have to admit he was real smooth. He extended his hand to the girls as I introduced them. They were such the little ladies. They both said, "Nice to meet you. Now can you take us over there to play?" We both laughed. Terry said sure as he held both of their hands and walked them to the play area, which was literally right behind where the officer had seated us, but you had to walk around this small wall barrier. He pulled some of the toys out of the chest for them, and they were off and running. The only times they returned to our table was to tell me they had to use the restroom or that they were hungry. Terry and I just enjoyed each other's company while the girls enjoyed themselves. Terry was a little nervous about the last hour of the visit when the play area closed since then he would really be put to the test with the girls because they would be sitting at the table with us. I told him to just relax and be himself. He did just that. Trina was sitting in his lap in less than ten minutes. I still don't know if that was because she could feel Terry's goodness or if she was just relishing in her own love of men. She has loved men since she was a little baby. Jada is much more reserved like me. I hadn't told Terry this yet, but winning Jada over was the real test. She has a keener sense of people's characters than Trina does. It takes her longer to warm up to people and figure them out, but by the end of the day he had both of my babies in his lap. As our visit was nearing its end, I whispered to Terry that he had passed the test. I was only visiting one day this time because I didn't want to push too hard with Terry or the girls. I wanted their relationship to develop naturally, which of course takes time. The drive back home to Buffalo seemed like it took just a few minutes. I guess that's because I was floating up there somewhere on Cloud 9 the entire time.

The next time Terry and I spoke we began to talk seriously about a committed relationship—a marriage behind the walls. I suggested that we both write down all of our concerns, issues, pros and cons in a letter so we could express our thoughts uninterrupted. Out of the blue, in the middle of the conversation, I said, "Terry, I love you."

He said, "Oh, baby, I love you too." Then I immediately asked him why he hadn't said it first. He said that he was insecure and fearful that I didn't feel the same way about him, so he allowed his fear to hold him back from speaking what was in his heart.

I let Terry know at that very moment that I walk by faith and not by sight or fear. I told him that fear and worry are not of God, and he should not operate in that vein. Here I was preaching to the man. I expressed to him the revelations of my prayers that had begun the day we met. I shared with him my belief that although we practiced religion differently, our prayers resonated with the same God. I told him that I believed that we were sent to each other from God. I believe that we are each other's blessing. This was the first and only conversation that Terry and I would share about God for many years. It was more comfortable for us to stay away from the topic of religion than to risk offending, hurting or alienating the other due to our ignorance of each other's beliefs and practices.

We agreed to mail our marriage concerns out to each other on a set date and not to talk until we saw each other the following weekend. I went to see Terry that Friday because the visiting room would be less crowded, so we could talk with fewer distractions and have three full days to talk everything out.

Our visit was deep to say the least. He had read and understood all of my concerns about the length of his sentence—he was still thirteen years from the parole board. Terry's sentence was twenty-five years to life, so the reality was that his freedom was never guaranteed. The financial aspects of this relationship even more so concerned me. How would we afford high phone bills and frequent visits? I questioned my own strength to be able to endure this for the long haul and the impact of everything on all of us. Terry had basically all of the same concerns I did. We talked through most of them. We held fast to our love, which in our eyes was our blessing from above and one from which we could not turn away. Terry asked me to marry him that very same day, and of course I said yes.

How do I love thee? On the day we said "I will," I felt alive. We had a very short but sweet Muslim wedding ceremony. I agreed to have a Muslim wedding ceremony because I only wanted to be married by a man of God. At the facility where Terry was, choices were pretty limited—we could either be married by a judge, or since Terry is Muslim the Iman could marry us. In the Islam faith believers say "I will" in their marriage vows, where in Christianity we say "I do." On this day we became one. It was no longer him and me—it was us. Terry kissed me—I mean really kissed me, not on my cheek, but on my lips, tongue and all. His kisses made me sparkle; I saw stars shining brightly in my eyes each time he kissed me. I know I've said it before, but this was really magic. I was truly the happiest woman alive.

Life was so blissful during the next four years. We learned so much about love, marriage and compromise. We exercised patience as we moved through our marriage and the correctional system as one. We discovered so much more about each other—how we react to situations and certain emotions. He laughed the first time he saw me cry while watching a movie. I caught him many times watching me as I slept. We were consumed with our family and surviving the odds. We were not going to be another prison marriage dissolution statistic.

We had a wonderful time developing our family. Terry was the best father to the girls. If I had handcrafted him myself he would not have been more perfect. The best day of Terry's life as a father was when the girls called him Daddy for the first time. Terry and I had been married almost a year. We were on our third family visit in the trailer that we'd call home for the next forty-four hours. The trailers were pretty nice. They were fully furnished two-bedroom apartments. They had TVs, VCRs and tons of movies to occupy the time. Terry was bouncing the girls on the bed and Jada said, "Daddy, don't let me fall." I was in the next room but I heard her. I walked to the bedroom where they were playing and saw the tears streaming down his face. He whispered to me, "Did you hear that?" I nodded. This was Terry's first Father's Day.

--- ❀ ---

"My beloved spoke, and said to me:

'Rise up, my love, my fair one, and come away.

For lo, the winter is past,

The rain is over and gone.

The flowers appear on the earth;

The time of singing has come,

And the voice of the turtledove is heard in the land.'"

—Song of Solomon 2:10–13

The Lord showed me love when He brought Rayna into my life. Our love experience is a shared one but our recollections connote different realities.

Yes, I did—I, Terry Williams, fell in love in an instant with this woman. I was, and still am, in awe of everything that she is and will be.

Living Separate Lives United Under One Love

Rhonda L. Harris

I stood there, as if in stealth mode, concealed by the shadow of the night, transfixed by the image of beauty laying there before me, unable to free myself, as though I were being held captive. She stirred, moving ever so gently under the sheet that barely covered her nakedness. Seeing her in such a vulnerable and inviting position activated the testosterone in my blood and my manhood. What was a brother to do? Instead of ravishing her, I continued to stand there admiring this magnificent human being with whom God Almighty has blessed me. Then suddenly, as if a magic lightbulb popped on, I wondered, *How did I ever get here?*

It's safe to say that it wasn't easy, and I for damn sure didn't get here all by my lonesome. I do know this much. I remained in that fixed position for a moment longer, contemplating this not-so-confusing thought. Because had things gone differently so many years ago, I would not be standing here asking myself this question. Doing time allows you a lot of time to think. I've often wondered and asked myself these same rhetorical questions, never really seeking an answer 'cause that would be crazy, right? However, there are those rare moments when I even surprise myself by blurting out a random thought or two. Don't worry, y'all, I ain't crazy. Well maybe crazy in love. As I remain standing here mesmerized by the reflection of Rayna's pronounced beauty, I know exactly how and why I arrived at this juncture in my life. I fell in love. It seems as though it was only yesterday that I met, fell in love and married this beautiful blossoming flower. Yeah, she's my forever beaming sunshine of life—that's what she is to me.

Rayna has shown me how to embrace and greet each day with open arms, a warm heart and a welcoming smile, because this is what she's been doing for the last fifteen years of our marriage. On the worst of days, be it dark-smeared black-blue clouds that block the sunshine and its warmth, she still manages to exemplify her gracious style. It is her spirit and love that helps guide me through my own murky days. She is my godsend. She is the force that drives me. She is my focus. She is my balance. *Ella es mi Reina*—she is my queen. It's no coincidence that Allah bestowed this woman as a blessing to me, and I thank Him and praise Him every day. As the wind stirred outside the trailer, I turned to stare out the window to see how far I could see. This is a view that I have embraced a million times since being confined. What I see right now is the brightly lit stars as I daydream about the day Rayna and I met.

Suddenly, my thoughts were interrupted by movement behind me. It is my queen getting up from her beauty rest, which she doesn't need because she's already so gorgeous. She is so stunning. For a few more seconds, I remained in the shadows until I saw the sheet slip completely off Rayna, revealing her voluptuous naked body. I smiled to myself and thought, *Now that's what I'm taking about.* Just as I was about to make my way around the couch to get to her, she stopped me dead in my tracks. "Down, boy," she said. "I have to go the ladies' room, and then I want to make us something to eat, if that's okay with you."

Dazed, I silently screamed to myself, *What the fuck? Doesn't she see that I'm ready to go again? Ladies' room? Something to eat? Still sore?* Hearing her say the words *something to eat* just put me in a trance. I started to salivate, thinking about eating her, especially with her naked ass standing there. I looked at her exposed mound with my moist tongue hanging and ready to fire away. I wanted to eat her. Seeing that look in my eyes, she said, "I'm serious, baby." I was thinking she must be mad. Didn't she not see me standing there at fucking attention? I must have had that look on my face that a child has when he's lost his favorite toy. Somehow she always knew what I was thinking, even at times like this. In all of our married years, I still haven't figured how this woman did that shit. Was I that predictable? Picking up on my feeling-rejected vibe, she leaned in and blessed me with a soft yet passionate kiss, as well as giving some modest hand caressing attention to "Mr. Attention," attempting to soothe a brother. Sensing my anticipation of progressing farther, she gently pulled away from me, saying, "Later, my love. You can have all of me later." The only words that I could muster up were "You're going to pay for this shit." Walking off to the ladies' room, she smiled mischievously as she seductively stuck out her tongue at me and closed the door behind her. I smiled and turned back to the window. I looked up above as though I could see where God's throne was, and I silently shouted, "Thank you, Lord, for giving me my soul mate."

The first time I saw Rayna was when she came into this room that was designated by the prison officials to take pictures. I was immediately attracted to her and her beauty. I could tell just by looking at her that she was a fascinating woman. She was the first woman who ever made a brother weak in the knees without even exchanging a word with me. Good Lord. I could not believe how I was reacting because nothing like this had ever happened to me during any photo sessions. I can honestly say that this shit caught me off guard. I was always the master of my domain when it came to women—at least I thought I was. For me, it was always the other way around. I made women weak in the knees. But this was different—Rayna was different. I had worked in this same picture room for years, and nothing of this magnitude had ever happened.

Rayna was beautiful beyond words. She was sexy and intoxicating. I just could not stop staring at her. Rayna's outfit was a perfect fit. She wore a bright yellow sheer silk shirt that enhanced her mahogany-colored skin, which complemented her fancy styled brown hair. Her pants were off white and kinda tight and graced her curves all too well. Even today when I look at my baby's ass, the only thing that comes to mind is that she is all mine. I ain't into sharing my baby with no other brothers—or sisters even for that matter for those who like to swing that way. Damn.

Sorry to digress but you know how it is when you just get lost in the moment. Back to what I was saying. Rayna is beautiful beyond the limited amount of makeup she wears to the details of her nails. The first day I saw her, she had on a pair of designer sandals that I didn't notice at first because I was too busy looking at her brightly painted red toenails. As beautiful as she was, she had pretty feet too. I'm not superficial, y'all, but I can relate to what Eddie Murphy was going through in *Boomerang*. I mean how would it look for a beautiful woman, fine as all outdoors to just up and reveal her charred heeled hooves attached to her jammed-up toes that she probably wanted you to suck after being tucked up in some too-small shoes all day? That just ain't right. That isn't for me—I ain't the one. Really I'm not superficial at all. I just want my woman to be beautiful inside and out—from her head to her toes.

I just could not stop staring at her. What was going on with me? All kind of shit was happening. My stomach got all queasy. Don't tell me you don't know what I'm talking about. We've all encountered someone who made us feel butterflies in our stomachs. I felt like she had put some kind of spell on me. The real icing on the cake was that I had the meanest hard-on that would not go away. Hey, I'm just being real here. That shit has never happened to me before in all of the years that I'd been in that photo room. I just could not control my desires for this woman. She sent my entire being in a tailspin, and my emotions were in an uproar—and she hadn't even spoken to me. My heart felt such a jolt that day that even to this day, so many years later, I am still unable to fully describe that wonderful experience. I guess I'm not supposed to.

Was I falling in love? Why now? Was Allah telling me something? He had to be. Of all the women that I've shot through the camera's lens time and time again, I'd never felt an attraction to any of them. And then "it" happened. The second our eyes met, a silent introduction occurred. I instantly knew that something magnificent had just taken place. I believe she knew it too. There was this unforeseen energy passing between us. I saw its recognition in her eyes. I knew this was special and something was sure to materialize between us. I just knew that something was bound to come out of this. When that would be or how that would be, I didn't know yet, but I knew that this would not be the end. I recalled a quote I read once that said, "Opportunity once forsaken is opportunity lost forever." I knew that I would have to seize the moment or remain lost forever. How was I able to make such a determination based solely upon a few minutes of visual contact? There are some things you just know. That day I knew that I would never look at another woman the way I looked at her. Even though the environment and circumstances weren't ideal for either of us, the feelings within our minds and hearts were. We were already in unison emotionally.

Today as I am sitting here on the couch watching her sashay around the kitchen, I am still in awe. Rayna is everything that I wanted in a woman and some of the things I wasn't sure I wanted. She is beautiful inside and out. My Rayna is just that woman. Her style is impeccable and her character is too. I've encountered many women in my life, and none of them have even come close to her caliber. She is the total package. Rayna is the fusion of beauty, power, determination and femininity. Simply said, she's a beautiful lady, and no other female has ever made me stand at attention the way she did that day.

Have you ever had a surge run so deep within you and feelings so intense that it stirred your very soul? That occurred when Rayna and I connected that very first day. I had to tell my brain what my heart already knew—I was falling in love. When she looked at me, it was like she could see straight into the depths of my soul and detect that I needed rescuing. I could see the very same things in her soul being revealed to me.

Unbeknownst to us both, she was my missing rib. She would change and reconstruct my life forever. She is my flower that bloomed and came alive in a prison picture room. Whoever said flowers don't bloom in the moonlight never knew my boo.

While Rayna was waiting for the individual she'd come to visit, I took the liberty of trying to regain my composure by calming myself down a bit. I think she saw me sweat enough. Although my nerves were on edge, I didn't want to let this chance pass me by, especially because I felt such an intensity and constant palpitations within my heart. I just felt that Rayna was my lifeline to forever happiness, and I couldn't let her slip through my fingers.

As I watched Rayna standing next to the painted mural in the photo room, I noticed that she was somewhere around five-two or five-three, a few inches shorter than myself, which was perfect for me. I knew we would definitely look good together as a couple. There she stood, not even ten feet from me yet I remained speechless even after the silent acknowledgement that passed between us. I hesitated because I knew that what had already transpired was considered a real no-no by prison standards, let alone by my Muslim religious beliefs, since there have been many scraps behind prison walls over something so small as a shared look between an inmate's female visitor and an inmate who showed interest. My only interest was to either give my info to her or to receive hers so that one of us could get the ball rolling, so to speak.

Yeah, I was neglecting all of the rules and morals to accomplish the one goal—to get Rayna. As I was sitting there just watching her, I was also thinking about this scene that happened a few years back to another camera man who overextended himself to a female visitor—the same act in which I was about to partake. The guy passed his name and number to this female because he said she gave him the okay to do so. When she came back to the desk to pick up the pictures, he had slipped his info between the photos. Well her husband, the inmate, found the slip of paper first and the drama began. The brothers had words in the visiting room. Of course the wife denied giving the other guy any indication that this was what she wanted, so the war between these two brothers began. The husband in that situation was an associate of mine. He expressed how embarrassed he was by what had gone on, and he vowed to not let the matter just die. Now the other guy thought that it is done and over with a week later when there'd been no more talk about what happened. He was still hoping that somehow, someway she would still write. He was too busy wondering what was taking her so long to get in touch with him that he didn't pay close enough attention to the matters at hand. I admit he wasn't the sharpest knife in the drawer. It was a hot Saturday afternoon, and we were in the yard playing basketball. All of a sudden a scuffle broke out on the court. Two players starting to beef over a call that was made by the defending player. Remember this is prison ball, and there are no referees. The two players started a pushing and shoving match, which got the COs' attention. Now the guy who tried to approach my man's wife was sitting on the sidelines just watching the commotion going on out on the court. The reality of the situation was that the fight on the court was an intentional distraction created by the husband so the COs wouldn't be watching what was going on on the sidelines. And that's when it happened. In less than five seconds, the other guy was cut bad. His face was slashed wide open because he disrespected his fellow inmate and his wife on the visiting floor. He got a bucfiddy, prison vernacular for a hundred and fifty stitches for that underhanded shit he pulled. I kept telling myself, *I'm not going out like this clown,* so I had to think clearly. I tried to stop staring at Rayna, so I looked down at the desk pretending to be busy. When I lifted my head back up, Rayna was looking directly at me. I couldn't think, let alone think clearly. There went my rule of conduct right out the window. I just couldn't help myself when it came to her, and the most confusing thing about all of this was that I didn't care about any of the potential repercussions. All I wanted to do was be in her presence just a bit longer to drink in her beauty before she left me forever.

She started to say something to me but never had the chance to get the words out because the brother she came to see walked through the door. When I saw who she was with, I was shocked beyond all belief. I looked over at her, astonished. I then looked at him thinking, *I know she is not coming up here to see you.* No way. I knew this cat, and he was a crab. I don't say that lightly. When I said, I knew this cat, I mean that I really knew him. He bunked in the same block that I did. He was just rubbing shoulders with some homo in the block—and when I say "rubbing shoulders," I really mean that they were probably rubbing much more than that. I begged silently, *Please smell the homo stench on him.* I'm not one for slinging mud on another brother but the truth is the truth. This guy was downright deceitful and disrespectful to men and women. I just knew that she couldn't really be feeling this cat. I was even more determined to get her. I had to find out what she saw in him; why was she visiting him. I couldn't overstep my boundary, so I waited for the right opportunity. I sat there watching them take pictures, getting more pissed off by the moment. I had to sit there tight lipped and watch him put his arm around her shoulder, as she reluctantly permitted … Wait. Did she flinch when he tried to cuddle up close to her? She had to. Or was my mind playing tricks on me because I was hoping for the worst to come out of this situation? Out of the blue, Rayna said, "Take the rest by yourself." Maybe she sensed my dissatisfaction when I saw him touch her. Why was I getting all upset because she allowed him to put his arm around her? After all, he was who she came to see. Why did she flinch when she noticed my disapproval? I was so disturbed by all of this that I was even more determined to stick to my original plan of getting Rayna all for myself. I know some of you may feel that I was wrong for my actions, and I can understand that, but for those of you who have fallen in love in an instant like I had then you, too, will understand the rationale for my actions. Let me not sugarcoat it. I just said to myself, *Fuck it. I'm moving full steam ahead.*

Now I was the other guy sitting there trying to figure out my options. I contemplated on how to pass this small piece of paper to Rayna with my information on it. I damn sure wasn't going to place it in between the photos because that's how that shit blew up in the past. I wasn't even worried about having a beef with Shawn if shit went haywire because my status was solid, and he wasn't well liked anyway, so I had no worries about him trying to pull the ball game shit on me. It did bother me though that I had to resort to using underhanded tactics to get at Rayna, but I managed to carry out my task quite respectfully. When their photo shoot was over, Shawn left the photo room before she did. His departure allowed me to conquer the spoils left behind. As I watched Shawn disappear in the shadows of the hall, I knew I had to act quickly before Rayna disappeared from the room.

Instead of Rayna bidding me adieu, she retraced her steps and headed to where I was sitting behind the desk. I wish you could have seen me. Right at the pinnacle of my moment, I got stuck on stupid. I was totally speechless. We were no more than a few feet apart when her hand brushed mine. She took the piece of paper with my name and number on it. I was shocked she really took it. I suddenly heard her angelic voice saying something like, "Hello, Terry. My name is Rayna" or "Nice to meet you, Terry. I'm Rayna." I was too excited to remember which. Her voice truly drew me even closer. I really couldn't stop staring at her. Her radiant beauty had become superimposed right before my very eyes. She was right there in front of me. I was going for mine. I knew at that moment that we were destined to be together. Rayna had become my future, and I hers. I was nervous and elated because what had just transpired between us within those few minutes gave me the epiphany that I would make Rayna the total focus of my life.

Now I knew her first name and that she had the most tantalizing voice I'd ever heard. I mumbled something to her about what her last name was. That's when I saw the most beaming and heartfelt smile I'd ever seen in all the years that I've been walking this earth. I kid you not. Her smile was unparalleled to anyone that I knew. She told me that we had the same last name. I smiled so deeply after hearing her soft, sweet words. I knew I was making the right choice even if that meant that I was going against my religious and ethical principles. Looking at her smile and feeling the warming effect it had on me, I knew that I would do anything to bring happiness into her life. My main concern was whether she would run far away from when she found out that I was in prison for murder.

When I retuned to my cell, I replayed the photo room encounter over and over and over, thinking about what I would say to Rayna in my first letter. I knew that I would focus on conveying things about me that would be of interest to her, rather than trying to impress her with some bullshit. I had every intention on telling Rayna the truth about everything. As I lay there, I also wondered what Shawn said to her to make her come see him. He was such a nefarious dude. He was the true epitome of evil, in my opinion. I used to watch this cat and just shake my head at the craziness that went on around him, always wondering if there would ever come a day when he would wake up. He had girls and homos bringing him drugs. He was supposed to be selling drugs but ended up using more than he sold. He would buy drugs from other cats knowing that he had no way to pay for them. He was always in deep shit. Now I'm not judging Shawn. I'm just making an observation. At the moment, I wasn't in a position to judge. I was a brother living in a glass house throwing stones. From the time I entered prison, I had strived to be a better human being, irrespective of my environment, which was accompanied by serving Allah to the best of my ability, but at that moment, I wasn't too sure how He viewed my behavior.

Two days had passed since my encounter with Rayna. I was lying motionless in my bed calculating how long it would take for her letter to arrive. If my timing was right I would be receiving it in a day or two. The mail only takes two days tops no matter where in New York you live. Hey if she was from the city the mail would get to me even sooner. Suddenly my feelings of elation were beginning to shift to concern. I started to worry that Rayna might have had second thoughts about writing me the moment she left the building that day, but she hadn't. Two days later the CO handling the mail run handed me a thick envelope with Rayna's name on it. My first instinct told me to savagely rip the envelope to shreds and dive right in to see what she wrote, but I didn't. Instead, I held on to it as gently as possible, fantasizing that this simple letter was her soft delicate hands, which I held just days before, in my very own. I had this huge smile, especially now that I had her letter. I just sat there on my bed staring at the envelope. I noticed how neatly she had written each letter in my name. You notice the small detail of things when you're not used to seeing them daily. For me, it was more than just having a perfumed letter in my hand; it was a confirmation as to what was to come.

As I carefully opened her letter, my attention was instantly drawn to the most enchanting fragrance. I had only smelled this one other time before. She wore it the day we met. Within a matter of minutes, her scent intoxicated my senses in a very comforting way as it continued to dominate the air in my humble atmosphere around me; it also carried her warm, gracious spirit. Thrilled to be smelling her fragrance once more, I brought the letter as close to my nose as possible and took a heaving whiff of it. All I could think about was how her scent overpowered me, and that was just from the paper. I sat there wondering how I would react once I had my arms around her and my nose in the crook of her neck. I was getting ahead of myself. I hadn't even read the letter, and I already had her hemmed up.

I read Rayna's letter through and through that day, a dozen times to be exact. I could tell that she was smart as a whip. To be quite honest, her letter blew me away. Each time I read her words, I became more attached to the author. Her words and sentences were flawless. I realized that I was not dealing with the average woman. Rayna was definitely intelligent, bright, confident and of course extraordinary in every way possible. She was surely no ghetto girl. Her level of intelligence was so well pronounced that I questioned my own. Yeah, her shit was tight.

The composition and electrifying approach of her first letter alone identified to me that she was passionate. She was committed to excelling, not only in academics but in every endeavor that demanded her attention. She was focused on overall success. I was truly impressed with her zest for education and excellence. She took the cake, in every fashion. I immediately tipped my hat to her—she was a strong black woman. I knew that a woman of her stature had to make many sacrifices in order to become the woman I'd met. Thinking about Rayna also made me think of my mother. I recalled watching my mother take care of and provide for me, my brothers and sister while working and maintaining a household. Rayna seemed to be no different. She was a beautiful, ambitious, intelligent and independent career woman. She was the devoted mother of two darling baby girls. Above all, she was dynamic. I immediately adored her. I admired her passion for education toward always striving to better oneself. Although I had been in prison for most of my adult life, I always looked for opportunities to learn and better myself. Education is so empowering.

My mother instilled this same fever for education and excellence in me as well. I will forever be grateful to her for it. She once told me that education is the key to excellence. I always wanted to share this same vision with my own children, if I ever had any. I would explain to them that a good education is not to be taken lightly because there are enough uneducated people running around this world, and I didn't want them following suit. As I pondered my mother's timeless wisdom, I looked toward my future with Rayna. Maybe someday I would get to make my speech to Rayna's daughters, if they'd become my daughters. I knew I was getting ahead of myself again, but clearly I just knew. I knew that this woman was definitely going to reshape me in every way.

Along with these aforementioned qualities, Rayna's lifestyle sort of emulated my mothers. My mother was a strong black woman who took no shit from anyone. She exerted her strength when she needed to. I could see that in Rayna, too, by some of the things she wrote. I admired Rayna's serious dedication to excellence and rising above any and all obstacles that were placed before her. I had such feelings of optimism about Rayna. Something within my heart told me that she would always rise and be just fine. She had a strong will to succeed.

When I read that she was a practicing Christian, I was instantly overcome with trepidation, because she was unaware of my religious beliefs. At that very moment, I wondered how she would take the news when I informed her that I was Muslim. Back then when people thought of Muslims they would think about Farrakhan, brothers in bow ties selling newspapers on the corners and terrorism. The truth though is that Islam is a peaceful religion. It has changed my entire life. Islam also respects other religious denominations, which was exactly what I was going to do with Rayna's. I wasn't scared because she was Christian. I was fearful that she would have reservations about us being able to make a spiritual connection, but I welcomed the challenge to overcome this and any other obstacles that might arise.

I had hoped that once I expressed myself about my religion that she would respect my beliefs. I thought about many of my Muslim brothers who had also married outside the faith. As long as she believed that there was no deity worthy of worship other than Allah, then we would be fine. From what I had read,

I believed that she was an open-minded person and would understand about the religion and understand me. She indicated in her letter that God was the most important factor in a relationship—without spirituality you have nothing. I knew that the sooner Rayna and I confronted this issue the better so I began writing my letter to her. I was lying in bed under the midst of darkness, staring up at the ceiling with Rayna's hypnotically sweet-smelling memento in my hand, unable to sleep. I tried to respond to her letter earlier but I couldn't because I was still so overwhelmed by the profoundness of hers. Each time I would start to put my collective thoughts on paper, I would stop and reread the first few lines and then become disappointed. I didn't want to come too eager, and I still had to tell her the painful things. But how did I share difficult and intricate details of my life story—especially the story detailing an introduction into prison—with someone I'd just met?

I knew that I had to be delicate. I knew that this was an once-in-a-lifetime shot for me, and I wasn't about to screw it up trying to pull the wool over her eyes. During the wee hours of the morning, I began writing. Even though the worry never went away, I continued to write. Even though I knew she might reject me once she found out that I used to sell drugs and then broke the cardinal rule of drug dealing by using my own product, which subsequently caused me to become a convicted murderer, I continued to write. I was worrying about everything at that point, but I persevered.

After mailing off my first letter to Rayna, it felt like an eternity while I waited for a response. I kept telling myself not to worry because Rayna said in her letter that she was understanding and didn't pass judgment on others. I tried to relax a bit, but not too much. The only thing that could have relaxed me would have been my reading her response to my letter. I felt like lightning had struck me twice. I really needed to know what Rayna was thinking and feeling about me whether good or bad. I felt like I could handle whatever her response would be because it was coming from her. I was just in awe of her. I was still a nervous wreck, but that night I humbled myself to God and prayed with a sense of urgency unlike any other prayer that I have ever made before. I literally begged Him to turn her heart toward mine because I needed to reshape my already fragmented life. The way I felt about the connection I believed I had with Rayna, this could only be His doing. The next day her letter arrived. When I opened it, I couldn't believe my eyes.

When I received Rayna's phone number in her follow-up letter, I was ecstatic. Yes, I thanked the Lord above. He heard me, like He always does. My personal prayers of thanks had also gone out to Rayna—thousandfold for not running away from me, but hopefully toward me. Now I had some new worries, but they were good ones. What was I going to say to her on the phone? Was I going to clam up like I had in the picture room? Was this a test to see where my head was at? Would she be able to detect the nervousness in my voice? My mind was reeling with so many different thoughts that it felt as if I were actually twirling in circles. The excitement I felt was extraordinary, and it was all because of Rayna.

The minute I heard her charming voice, my heart started to beat five times quicker. Her voice was so soothing. It stimulated my entire being as well as restoring my confidence. We shared so much with each other during our first phone conversation that we both felt the closeness developing between us. There was no need to inquire as to whether this was real. With every telephone call and letter we exchanged, our connections and feelings grew. There was so much positive growth going on that we began to surpass even our own expectations of what was happening between us. I was undeniably falling in love with her.

During one of our conversations, I wanted so desperately to ask her to come visit me, but I chickened out before I could formulate the words. Then another day came and I just asked her flat out, "Would you come visit me?" I wanted to have the chance to gaze upon her beauty as I listened to her melodic voice while her words penetrated my ears and heart simultaneously. It wasn't about seeing her for the purpose of lusting over her. My intention was solely to make an indelible impression upon her, as she had done with me. More than anything, I wanted her to look into my eyes so she would take notice that there was much more than just friendly interest in them for her. What I felt was more like my want, need and desire to make a marriage investment that would yield a togetherness lasting us a lifetime.

The rumor mill had a field day with the news of our first visit. Shawn approached me about it but there was no beef. I had saved his ass from beatdowns far too may times for him to come at me from any other angle than that of mutual respect. He gave me the pictures that he and Rayna had taken on that day and said, "I guess the best man won" and walked away. We never spoke about this again.

On our first visit, the conversation was more than just pleasant. It was revealing and refreshing, if I say so myself. She was truly elegant as she sat there before me. Yeah, I said elegant—even in a prison. She outshone everyone in the room. I couldn't stop staring at her while we talked. We found out that we had so much in common. I kept harping on how much we resembled my parents. My father once told me, "If you ever find a woman possessing qualities like your mother, marry her." While Rayna continued to share her life story with me, I was sitting picturing the two of us jumping the broom. Before we knew it, it was just five minutes before visiting hours would come to an end. As I helped her with her coat, I wanted so badly to kiss the softness of her heart-shaped lips, but I suppressed this feeling. My Muslim faith prohibits overstepping the boundary lines by engaging in physical contact with a sister that is not your wife. Rather than respond to my lower desires, I kissed her upon her cheek as I said good-bye. My reasoning was simple and hopefully forgivable by God. My sole intention was to make Rayna my wife.

Walking away from Rayna, I knew without a shadow of a doubt that she would be the only woman I would ever love and take as my wife as long as I lived. She had now become a part of me, as I became a part of her.

People say that there is no such thing as love at first sight.

I used to believe this was true until it happened to me.

The only difference is that instead of love at first sight, mine was love at first read.

—*Anise*

Love Recognizes No Barriers

Susan Goins-Castro

"Love recognizes no barriers It jumps hurdles, leaps fences, penetrates walls to arrive at its destination, full of Hope!"

—*Maya Angelou*

Five years, two months. That's how long we've been at this thing that we've got. It's not always easy, but it's so good that at times, it often feels like we're the only people who have something truly real.

It all began with a letter I wrote back on February 28, 2001. Never in my wildest dreams could I have imagined that I was about to write to the person who would one-and-a-half years later turn out to be my husband.

As I stated earlier, it all began with a letter that I sent to Geo. That's his name Geovanni. At the time, I was involved in a relationship, but it wasn't anything serious. It was more about having fun and very casual because I had just come out of a long term relationship and the guy I was seeing was just coming out of a bad marriage. I can honestly say that when I first wrote to Geo, it was more so out of boredom. I knew this girl who was dating a man in prison, and she came to me one day and asked me if I was interested in writing to her man's friend.

I often think back to that day, and it reminds me that Geo and I were an act of faith. The girl told me that she would send my name and address to Geo so that he could write me, but I was too impatient. I felt something from the very beginning, and we hadn't even contacted each other yet.

I remember writing him an introduction letter and then waiting daily for the mailman to bring me a reply. After about two weeks, I began to think that I wasn't going to hear from him, but then one day while I was checking my mail, there it was—a letter from the Clinton Correctional Facility. I was so excited that I was barely able to open the envelope.

It was a very nice introduction letter. He told me a little about himself, his daughter and about some of the things he did daily to pass the time. I wrote him back immediately. I told him about my children and about things that I still wanted to achieve in life.

In his next letter to me, he explained he was incarcerated because of armed robbery and his hopes that this wouldn't affect us being friends. Again, I wrote him back immediately and explained that I wanted to continue getting to know him.

From that point, things took off. I wrote him daily, and I received a letter from him each day. By April, my feelings for him were changing. I was experiencing something a lot stronger than friendship, but I wasn't really sure how he was feeling about me.

Geo and I had grown quite close in those few months. We wrote each other about everything. We talked about past relationships, our families and our dreams. He was so easy to talk to and always very encouraging. I felt like we had known each other for years instead of only a couple of months. I opened up to him about things that I had never told another soul. That's just how close we had become.

Sometime around the middle of April, I received a letter from Geo telling me that he was going down to court in the Bronx and that I might not hear from him for a while but that he was going to try to keep in touch as much as he could. He said that I could continue to write him because his mail would follow him. I decided to make sure that I wrote him at least twice daily just to make sure that he had some mail while he was away.

It was during this time that I realized just how much I cared for him. I began thinking about us having more than a friendship and how this would be able to work. I wrote to him about the way I was feeling and tried to get a sense of what his feelings were for me. When I didn't hear from him, I felt like such I fool. I thought I had scared him off by admitting what was going on in my heart.

My biggest fear about getting involved with him was our age difference. I was thirty-four, seven years older than him. I really didn't pay any attention to his age until I began to fall in love with him. I wrote to him about my concerns and the fact that I had four children from my previous relationship.

I also debated about how a relationship with someone who was incarcerated would work. And let's not forget that technically, I was involved with someone already.

Besides the things that I wrote to Geo about, I had to wonder if being in a relationship with a person who was incarcerated was something that I could really do. The last thing I wanted was to hurt him by changing my mind in a couple of months. During this time, I did a lot of soul searching and praying. I also read a book called *The Prisoner's Wife*. That book gave me a lot of insight as to some of the things that I could expect. It also let me know that I could do this relationship and that there were other women doing the same thing.

When Geo returned from court and wrote me, I was so relieved. He hadn't been ignoring me at all. None of my letters had been forwarded to him—they were waiting for him upon his return. He addressed all of my concerns, and the main thing that stuck out in my mind was the comment he made that regardless to his age, he was still a grown man. That was the last conversation we ever had about our age difference.

We had our first date in June. This was a phone conversation. I remember answering the phone and then hearing the message begin: "This is MCI. You have a collect call …" I was so nervous and excited that I was barely able to breathe. When he said hello and I heard his voice for the very first time, I thought that I was going to pass out. His voice was like music to my ears. He sounded so smooth that it was intoxicating.

Things moved pretty quickly between us after that. By August, I knew that I was going to marry this man one day. He had brought so much into my life in such a short period, more than any other man had ever done before. He gave me comfort and support when I needed it. Meeting him made me realize that he had all the qualities that I wanted in a man. I still wasn't sure how this was going to work, especially with him having a sentence of twenty-two years to life, but I also knew that I had to somehow make him mine.

One day in October while we were talking on the phone, Geo told me that he had purchased an engagement ring for me. He said that it was more of a promise of his love because he really didn't want to ask me to marry him while he was still in prison. He told me some years later when we were talking about it, that he felt had he asked me to marry him then, that it may have scared me off.

Even though he didn't actually ask me to marry him that day, us having this conversation basically gave me an idea of the direction that our relationship was headed. As soon as we hung up the phone, I began stressing and felt very confused. I was experiencing all the things that I felt in the beginning of our relationship when I was trying to decide how to go about us becoming more than friends. I thought about my children's father and what I would do if he were to come back into my life. Would I take him back? Did I even want to? Did I really think that I was going to have the happily-ever-after ending with Geo serving time in a correctional facility? I had so many new questions now that the subject of marriage had come up. I did some long, hard soul searching about the possibility of us getting married. Even though I knew months ago that I would marry him one day, I really hadn't considered the fact that it might take place while he was still incarcerated. I thought about him. I thought about me. I thought about my children and how they might feel about the situation. They knew of Geo and had spoken to him on the phone from time to time when he called, but marriage was a whole different story.

I needed to make sure that I could truly handle this lifestyle because that's what it is, a lifestyle. I had so many fears and doubts about how we would be able to survive this because I didn't want us to be another statistic of a failed prison marriage. But even with all the thoughts and questions I had, never once did I question Geo's love and commitment to me.

I woke up bright and early one January morning and suddenly, everything seemed so clear. I no longer felt stressed or undecided. I knew that I could never love anyone the way I loved Geo and that he was my very best friend. He was the first person who came to mind for me to share things with good or bad. He was the one who was so loving, supportive, caring and comforting to me. I knew at that very moment that I was able to have this relationship with him and that I couldn't see my life without Geo being a part of it. I decided to trust and believe in the love that we had for each other and follow my heart. I wrote Geo a beautiful letter expressing my love and devotion for him and then asked him to marry me. Yes, you are reading correctly. Geo had me so open that he had sista girl asking him to marry her.

I received a letter from Geo a couple of days later in response to my marriage proposal. He said that this was a serious matter and that he would rather discuss this on the phone or in person.

Let me share a little secret with you now. Geo and I hadn't actually met in person. Can you believe that? Here I was asking this man to marry me and we had never met. We laugh about it now because we know that it sounds crazy. I guess that's the reason we've never shared this with anyone before.

Geo called about a week later, and we had the talk. He started off with, "Anise, you know my situation and the fact that I don't know exactly when I'll be coming home. I want to make sure that you really understand this and that you can handle it. Even though I have an appeal in, things may not go the way I hope and pray for. Would you be able to handle that?"

I then explained how much he meant to me and that regardless of the situation, I wanted to spend the rest of my life with him. I explained that I'd rather have him in my life even if we couldn't physically be together for now than to not have him at all. When we hung up after saying good-bye and I love you, I had a wedding to plan.

Our next step was to get permission from the superintendent to get married. Geo wrote the letter. Once he received the approval, I had to contact the family reunion coordinator to find out what the next steps were. I had to have an interview, which took place over the phone because of the distance that I lived from the facility.

He asked if I knew the reason why Geo was incarcerated and if I planned to come meet him before the wedding. I couldn't even get upset with the man for asking me that. I just answered yes to all of the above. I know that man thought I was crazy for wanting to get married without having met Geo. Yes, I was crazy—crazy in love. The gentleman explained everything that I needed to bring with me and the fees that were needed for the ceremony and license. Once I completed that call, Geo and I had a wedding date.

We didn't actually meet until that April and we were to be married in August. The only reason that we hadn't met sooner was because of the distance. At the time he was five hours away, and going to see him was like planning a major trip. I had to plan for transportation and hotel accommodations, make arrangements for my children to stay with my mother and take time off work.

The first time I went to see him, I took Greyhound. It took more than seven hours to get there. I left at 5:00 P.M. Friday and arrived at 12:30 A.M. I caught a cab to my hotel. While in the cab, I asked the driver how far the facility was from there, and he said about twenty minutes. He was still going to be on duty around the time that I wanted to go so I made arrangements with him to be picked up before I got to my hotel.

By the time I walked into my room and began to get settled, it finally hit me that I was really there and I was about to come face to face with the man of my dreams. I remember sitting in my room that night and trying to figure out if all this was really real. I wanted to go to sleep to make the time pass quicker but I was too excited to sleep. I finally drifted off sometime around 2:00 A.M.

I woke up extra early so that I could begin to get ready. I felt more like I was preparing for a big night out on the town. I had bought a new outfit and had my hair and nails done. After all, this was going to be our first official date. Geo and I had exchanged photos, but I have to admit, I was more than a little nervous about trying to pick him out of a crowd.

Once I arrived at the facility, it took about an hour to be processed because of the number of people. I had to take a number and they only processed five at a time.

When I finally arrived at the visiting room, I gave my pass to the corrections officer and was assigned to a table where I then proceeded to wait for Geo's arrival. I struck up a conversation with the woman sitting next to me and didn't even see when Geo came into the room. He saw me and came over to the table. I looked up when I noticed a figure out the corner of my eye coming toward me, and it was him. He was so handsome: jet-black hair, dark brown eyes and a body that looked like it had been chiseled out of stone. He gave me a big hug and a soft, friendly kiss. I was so nervous. I was hoping and praying that this man sitting across from me would be the same one who managed to make me fall in love with him through a letter.

Our conversation in person was relaxing and as easy as it had been from our letters and previous phone calls. Little did he know that I fell in love with him all over again that day. He had sent me money to get our wedding bands the previous month so I bought them along with me for him to see. We talked about our upcoming marriage and about some of the reasons why our relationship was so good.

The thing I remember most about that day is how Geo sounded just like the letters he had been writing me over the last year and a half since we met. Our first meeting assured me that I was making the right decision about our relationship.

It felt as though the time flew by because before I knew it, the announcement was made that visiting hours were over. At the end of the visit, Geo was able to walk over to my side of the table where he proceeded to really give me a hug. This is when we shared our first real kiss. It was magical. The perfect kiss. Not wet and sloppy. It also felt good to be held in his arms. I left the facility knowing that he was the one for me.

After that visit, I went up monthly but that was my last bus trip. I drove up instead. I would leave the house by 3:00 A.M. and arrive in Plattsburg by 8:00 A.M.

I had to go to the facility the day before our wedding to take care of the license so I didn't go up to visit in July. Our wedding was the beginning of August so I just waited until then.

I made the decision not to tell anyone that I was getting married. At the time, I felt that it was something a lot of people wouldn't understand, and I didn't feel like having to defend my relationship to anybody. Besides, I didn't want anyone trying to take my happiness from me. I already had people asking me questions like why I was dating an inmate, so saying I was going to marry him was going to cause a floodgate of new questions. The only people who knew I was getting married were my children, my cousin who is like a sister to me and one friend who served as one of our witnesses. I needed to bring someone with me so that I could have Geo's witness pulled out for a visit.

The next thing was to figure out what to wear. I decided on a simple dress. I had to make sure that I choose something that they would allow me to wear into the facility without a problem because they are very strict when it comes to the visitor's dress code. I ended up picking a white slip dress that had a sheer white overlay that had the sleeves I needed in order to get into the facility since they don't allow you to wear anything strapless. I found a beautiful clear sandal that made me feel like a princess on my special day. Just like Cinderella. And Geo was my Prince Charming.

It was finally time for our wedding. As I stated earlier, I had to come up the day before to take care of the license. I arrived at the facility, and at first I couldn't get in. I had gotten my hair done in an updo style that had bobby pins in it, so I was setting off the metal detector, and the correction officers wouldn't let me in. Now I was mad, crying and trying to explain that I was getting married the next day and had to get in to take care of my license; but they could care less. I then asked if they would call the family reunion coordinator whom I was suppose to be meeting so that he would know I was there, but they wouldn't even do that for me. I had to leave the facility to go purchase some shampoo and go back to my hotel room to wash my hair so that I could remove all the pins. I had so much hairspray in my hair that I couldn't just take the pins out.

By this time, it was noon, and I had to be back at the facility by 1:30 in order to get in. I was stressing because my hotel was about twenty-five minutes away from the facility. I also was worried that Geo would think that I had changed my mind and wasn't coming. I sped back to the hotel, washed out my hair and then pulled it into a ponytail. I didn't even have time to blow dry it. I did eighty miles per hour back to the facility with a soaking wet ponytail hanging down my back, wetting up my shirt, but I got back by 1:20.

Geo and I talked about that day in a later conversation, and he told me how that entire morning all the guys in his block were yelling and giving him well wishes, but when one o'clock came and he hadn't been called down for a visit, there was dead silence because everyone thought he had been stood up. I'm so glad that I was able to prove them wrong.

Our wedding took place the next day. I arrived at the facility around 10:00 A.M. to be processed and proceeded to the visiting room to wait for Geo. He arrived about twenty minutes later looking as handsome as ever in a brand-new white shirt he had purchased just for the occasion. We visited for a couple of hours until the CO came over to our table around one o'clock to inform us that they were ready to begin the ceremony. Our wedding took place in a little office off the visiting room. The entire thing was so quick. I didn't even realize that the woman performing it had begun. It took all of five minutes.

What stands out in my mind is the fact that his ring was a little tight and looked like it wasn't going to go on his finger but I was determined to get that ring on him. The vows were very emotional for me. I didn't cry. It's just that I felt them deeply in my heart. Here this man was promising to love and honor me, and he wasn't only saying it to me but he was saying it out loud for the entire world to know. Then the judge said, "I now pronounce you husband and wife. You may now kiss the bride." It was official. We were official.

We had to wait a few minutes while the witnesses signed everything so we stood there locked arm in arm, trying to take in and understand what had just taken place. We were actually married.

I was floating on air by the time we returned to the table. We only had about an hour to spend together, but I was coming back the next day before returning home. Geo and I spent the rest of the visit looking at each other and smiling. I couldn't believe that I was married, and I think he was feeling the same way.

When I got back to the hotel and changed out of my dress, I opened up a bottle of Moet to celebrate. I was so happy, but I was also feeling lonely. This was never the way I dreamed of getting married and spending my wedding night. I basically cried the entire night.

It was never out of regret though. I knew that I had made the right decision. I just felt so alone because I couldn't celebrate it with the people who meant the most to me, which was all of my family and friends, and I hated the fact that my new husband wasn't with me.

The next couple of months flew by with the kids going back to school in September and me visiting Geo monthly, and before you knew it, November had arrived and we had been married for three months. That meant that the time had come for us to begin working on our next project and that was getting family reunion visits or trailers as most people who don't have them call it. This is a program that if you are approved for, the prisoner is allowed to spend forty-four hours of private time in a designated area within the facility with his family. You have to be married ninety days before you can apply.

During this time, there was so much sexual tension between Geo and me. Before we got married, we used to write erotic letters. Once we got married, all the letters stopped. I guess that was due to the fact that our being together physically was about to become a reality, and it had both of us a little nervous.

Once we received approval for the family reunion program, I had to have my picture taken for his file. This would be used to physically identify me as his wife. We selected a date in January to have that taken care of. At first, the FRP coordinator asked if I wanted a weekend or a weekday so I said weekend. I figured that would be better and I would only have to take off one day from work but then he began flipping the book all the way down to the month of May to check availability, so I told him I would take a weekday instead. We got a date for six weeks later.

Geo and I decided that we didn't want to spend a lot of time cooking during our first private time together. During that time, you were allowed to bring already prepared food from the outside into the facility so I bought food from restaurants so that all we would have to do was warm it up.

Our honeymoon was scheduled for March 3. That was a Tuesday. Geo and I decided that we would call this our honeymoon instead of an FRP because it was special to us. I had to arrive at the facility by 9:00 A.M. Since the facility was so far away and this was a weekday, there was only one other couple going out that day, so it didn't take long to be processed. We were loaded up onto a van and taken into the facility.

I was actually surprised to see the trailers. They weren't what I had expected. I thought that they were going to look like real trailers. Instead they looked like little two-family houses. The officer told me and another woman who was also there which unit we were in then left to pick up the men. I walked around while I was waiting for Geo to arrive. It was actually a cute little place. It had two bedrooms, a kitchen and a living room.

While waiting for Geo, I began to have a lot of thoughts. I couldn't believe that shortly, after seven months, we were about to finally consummate our marriage.

I was staring out the kitchen window and daydreaming when I heard the door opening. I turned to see the CO coming in along with Geo. He was looking so good to me, even more handsome than he usually did. The officer was explaining where everything was and about how the count would be handled while we were on our honeymoon. We couldn't wait for the officer to finish so that he could leave.

When he left, Geo gave me a big hug, and we shared a long, passionate kiss. He took me by the hand and led me over to the couch where we shared some more kisses before he asked if I wanted to go lie down. I answered yes, and we headed off into the bedroom. Once we reached there, Geo began to undress me slowly.

All those months of talking trash to him had finally caught up to me. It was now time for the real thing, and I was scared to death. Not of Geo. I was just very shy about him seeing my body, and there he was undressing me. All those months I had my clothes to protect me and now he was about to see every flaw I felt I had.

When everything was off, I was trying to cover myself with the sheet, but he removed it and just looked at me. He began to tell me how beautiful I was and how much he loved me, and all those insecurities I was feeling disappeared.

He left no part of my body neglected. When he finally entered me, it was like we were made for each other. We had a rhythm like we had been together for years. Our lovemaking was filled with so much passion. After making love with Geo, I felt as though it was the first time I had ever had sex. He not only made love to my body but also to my soul.

Our time together during our honeymoon gave me an idea of how life would be once he came home. We showered together, and the man bathed me. I was in heaven.

Those forty-four hours seemed to fly by. We had spent such a wonderful time together, and it was over and time for me to leave. The van was supposed to pick us up at 8:00 A.M., so when they called Geo for count at 6:30 that morning I got up and began getting my things together. I was hurt and angry. I was angry at Geo for not being able to leave with me, and I was hurt because I had to leave him there.

I got into the shower alone and cried. I thought that I could get it all out in there and then be alright by the time I got out but that didn't happen. I cried while I got dressed and continued until I came out of the bedroom. I never knew that it would be so hard to leave him that day.

After everything was packed, we sat on the couch hugging and I began to cry again. The last thing I wanted to do was to cry in front of him. I turned my head away but he asked me to look at him. Geo told me that I didn't have to cry because things wouldn't always be this way and that I had to have faith that God was going to open up the doors for him to come home soon. I told him that I would but in my mind, I was wondering how I was supposed to do that.

We hugged until the phone rang for us to walk out to the gate to be picked up. We shared our last kiss, and I got onto the van to leave.

As I was riding down to the parking lot to begin my long trip home, the tears began to flow again. The burning question in my mind was no longer how I was going to get through this but if I even wanted to …

I never thought about the qualities I wanted in a man until you came along. I used to think that the only thing important was to have a man period. Now I know better, and that's all because of you.

—*Anise*

What Is the Definition of a Husband?

Susan Goins-Castro

He knows you better than anyone and loves you even when you don't really love yourself.

He supports you through the good times and the bad.

He believes in your ability to achieve your dreams and cheers you on when you feel that they may be slightly out of your reach.

He's your first thought in the morning and your last one at night.

He's the one who makes everything in life have so much more meaning and has you wondering how you managed before finding him.

He's the one who looks at you like you are the most beautiful woman in the world because that's how he honestly feels about you.

He's the one who passes on wisdom to your children and sets an example of what a man is for your sons and instills those same values in your daughters so that these are the same qualities they will look for in a man later in life.

He's the one who cries with you along with giving you comfort and reassurance to hold on to your faith when you lose your mother.

He's the one who can tell what you're thinking or feeling with just a glance.

He's the one you can see yourself growing old with.

He's the love of your life, your lover and best friend.

He's the reason that you believe in love again …

He is my husband.

My definition of a husband was not being defined by plans for a future together, it was staring our current reality in the face. Julius had served eight years already, and there was no guarantee for a quick release. I was stuck on the here and now, which was not all bad. Our journey didn't appear to be that charted course for smooth sailing, and our harmony came from above entered in creating peace and illuminated back out. Marrying in the best of times requires confidence and commitment; marrying in the "for worse" is a leap of faith.

I was choosing to share this ride with Julius. We were stepping out on faith.

—*Naomi*

Stepping Out on Faith

R.Y. Willingham

"Some journeys begin with the charted course and plans
for smooth sailing …
Wind at your back and the tide's harmony lulling you along the way.
Some journeys are leaps of faith with uncertainty on the horizon
and desire in the heart …
Full of favor and challenges of character drawing each closer to
the Creator's wisdom and purpose.
We choose this journey …"

—R.Y. Willingham

"Why these people keep on messing with me?" I asked as I read that Julius had just been transferred to yet another facility. It was two days after Christmas and three days before I was to be in New York. The tears filled my eyes, but they refused to fall.

We knew that Julius' medical hold would be released soon and he would have to relocate to another facility because his classification did not warrant his stay. Mrs. Carry had hoped and had some expectancy that Julius would not be moved until after the holiday. With all of Mrs. Carry's experience, we had relied on that to proceed with plans to marry on January 1.

It was a very cold day both outside and in my heart. That December, we had an ice storm that left much of the city without electricity for more than a week. Simone was to accompany me both for the drive and to be my witness on my wedding day. She stood in the dining room of my home, as I was angry again. This time, neither Julius nor I had anything to do with another missed wedding date.

The following morning, I called Mrs. Carry because she had always been a good listener and had a way of focusing on the bright side of the things that were happening with Julius.

"Hello, Mrs. Carry. This is Naomi Hill. How are you this morning?"

"Just fine. Thank you. You are aware that Julius has moved. Let me get the folder and I can tell you where he's headed," she said. She looked for a few moments and gave me a location. She also told me that it was a good place and that she knew he would be upset with having to miss the wedding date. I thanked her for her time and for telling me where his drafted location would take him, as I wouldn't know until his arrival and his facility location on the Department of Corrections' website had changed.

I laid my face on the dining room table, wrapping my arms around my head. I began to pray because I needed to know what God had in store, and more importantly I needed His comfort. "Lord, this time I was ready and committed to marry this man. I believed that you would bless this union and honor my faithfulness. I don't know what to think of this move. It was all in your hands. Are you telling me not to marry him?" If God was speaking to me that day, I didn't hear His voice nor did I feel comforted since January 1 had always been my ideal wedding day.

Julius wrote me while in transit and told me where he would be. I mapped out yet another road trip to a New York correctional facility. I became all too familiar with I-90 East. I was going to visit my friend, who should by that time have been my husband. I planned a future date of a couple of weeks from the present to visit so that he had time to settle. The only good thing I found about Julius' transfer was he was down to 370 miles away.

When I arrived at this new facility, I noticed the number of regular visitors. They are easily identifiable because they are greeted by the staff with familiarity. They all know the routine of the facility and many of the officers by name. I often wondered if they had assimilated to this lifestyle and how long it took. I was still rebelling against this human condition belonging to me. I was in it, but it was not a part of me.

I was anxious and frustrated upon my arrival. The entire drive, I had been accompanied by disappointment and discouragement. My experience of having plans being turned upside down had impacted me. This had nothing to directly do with his crime and everything to do with our circumstances. I loved Julius, unlike any love I had ever known. I had comfort in my Lord's words, but I still ached that we were not to be husband and wife on the first day of the year.

Every time I saw Julius, he looked even more handsome. I could see his attractiveness on the outside, but as time progressed I saw more qualities in him that I valued and wanted for myself. Julius joined me at the table with an embrace of immediate understanding. He began to talk about the new facility and the lack of programs that he had hoped for. He did not speak of our forfeited wedding date in the beginning moments of the visit. Instead, we were solely focused on the nature of programs—or lack thereof—in a New York facility. I disturbed his current business conversation with my question of "When are we getting married?"

Julius looked surprised, as if the relocation and passing of our previous date had completely changed my mind. As I looked into his eyes, I saw reservation, almost like he had experienced an omen or some type of superstition. Julius certainly had understood all of my previous concerns and fears, but what he didn't know was how protected I felt with him and how favored I knew our relationship to be. My peace that came in October during the fast had brought a covenant between God and me that was unwavering. I knew that my love for Julius was a godsend, and I also was beginning to believe that we could be a whole couple despite our current circumstances. Julius looked concerned, but he agreed to find out when we could get married. We both thought that it would come quickly and even considered Valentine's Day. We enjoyed the remainder of the visit and were resilient in our efforts to get married.

The following week, I received a letter from Julius. We would not get married until May. The new facility had weddings once a year. After speaking to his new counselor, I was told that most medium facilities were going to allow prison weddings once a year. According to Mr. Santiago, it was too much of an inconvenience to organize the weddings. I felt like a five-month delay was a life sentence, and I mourned that news like tomorrow would never come. Julius assured me that the time would come and go quickly, and we would soon be married. I began my countdown immediately, tickering every calendar I could find.

As the days rolled by, I wrote yet another letter to a superintendent requesting permission to marry Julius. It was a routine requirement and nothing I spent much time in doing.

Each time I had written that letter it said the same thing:

ᦕ

Dear Superintendent Whoever:

I am writing you to express my intent to marry Julius Whinston 96A0102. He is currently in confinement at whatever facility, and in accordance to the Directive #4201, I am required to inform you of this decision. Please begin the necessary processing to complete this request. Thank you.

Sincerely,

Naomi Hill

The only distinguishing factor of one letter from the other was the date, facility and the recipient's name. Everything was mechanical and outside of us, as if it didn't really belong to us. It was a formality for marriage in a prison, and I hated it. I did not give much credence to it because for me, Julius was in their care, but they did not have ownership of him. The reply came quickly as the other preceding two had. Our wedding date was the beginning of May. The only requirements for marriage were forty dollars for a license, another forty dollars for the justice of the peace and two witnesses for the day of the ceremony. We still needed our birth certificates for the license, and we could not have our own wedding vows. Everything was going to be uniform and run like any assemblyline. The only thing we had a contributing factor with was the two required witnesses. Julius did not mind who they were and left that decision to me.

I wanted our day to be blessed and surrounded by people who loved and supported us. I initially asked my brother, Alex, and his wife, Simone. Alex hurt me first by not providing a response at all. The worse hurt I could have felt was the lack of response which I interpreted to mean "no-reply needed or do not validate the question." Alex had in effect told me that my request was not even worth validating with a response. Simone had been more understanding and supportive throughout the development of my relationship with Julius. She had encouraged me with expressing how beautiful and wonderful what he and I had found was. However, she had to be indulgent from afar because her contribution to our wedding day would be the care of my son, Quincy, while I was away.

I wrote a list of who I would want to stand beside me in agreement and advocacy on our wedding day, and the list seemed so small. It was reduced to what I could count on one hand. The next people on my list were Myeisha,

Renata and Tia. Myeisha knew me the best and loved me the most. I asked if she would be my witness, and not much to my surprise, she sharply said, "No. I am not going into no prison." Her firmness and decisiveness cut me as quick as her words and as deeply as my brother's reply had done. I ached and ironically felt alone in my happiness, which felt like it was being chiseled into something ugly. I knew that Tia was not an option because her departure from home would leave undue stress on her husband. Renata was my single option and the person that I would have desired most because of her accompanying faith and prayers. I asked Renata, and her only spoken determining factor was the fact that it was the Friday before Mother's Day. Renata and her mother were inseparable, although they lived more than 160 miles apart. Missing Mother's Day would have been breaking the Eleventh Commandment—Thou shall not omit thy mother. I was required to have the information to the facility no later than two weeks before the wedding date so that the witnesses' names could be cleared to enter the facility. I asked Renata on more than two occasions, and at one point I felt that my invitation wasn't treated with any significance or notability; knowing that unlike in the free world, prison affords fewer choices and input of decisions being made. Our wedding was regulated by policies and procedures of that state facility. I felt that my request was unwanted and shut down.

Over the next few weeks, I became more isolated and angry with my friends and family. I thought back on wedding after wedding to which I had either contributed or supported the planning and preparation. I had played coordinator, floral designer, invitation preparer, reception decorator, phone tree administrator, pickup and delivery driver and most of all supportive friend. With just over a month before my wedding day, I had none of those people in my corner or even on my block. The isolation, abandonment and hurt created anger, and the anger perpetuated the isolation. Julius' only advice to me was, "Forget them." How do you forget? I didn't. I remembered, and I forged ahead on the fact that I knew that God had my back. I prayed for understanding, and I prayed for a forgiving spirit because I felt that none of my friends even tried to conceive what I was going through. I thought that God was answering my prayer with Renata's agreement to accompany me to New York to marry Julius. Our two witnesses were set. Dana and Renata would stand with Julius and me as we wed.

I had crossed off all the major items on my list: I had child care for Quincy, the two witnesses, money set aside for the hotel and travel expenses, as well as the license and justice of the peace fees. I had an idea of what I was to wear, until at Julius' request I decided on a more traditional off-white suit. I was ready and most of all calm.

Julius and I wrote over the next few weeks. I had not matched his frequency, and it caused concern for him. He didn't understand all of my errands and running around had caused some fatigue on my end. He feared that this wedding might not happen. His letters would start with "How are you doing out there?" or "Are you okay?" I would respond, but it would sometimes take me a couple of days just to tell him everything was fine. Julius was hopeful but not desperate. He bordered on "Are you still showing up?" but would have to trust our love.

We were down to two weeks before the wedding and the last day that all names had to be to the head counselor organizing the wedding day. Renata called me to meet her for lunch. It was a beautiful late spring day—sunny, warm and slightly windy. I arrived early, excited about my upcoming nuptials and the idea of my close friend being by my side. We would have fun after the ceremony that evening over dinner in the neighboring town.

We met in the food court of an upscale mall. Renata and I were opposites in many ways. She liked Mexican, and I wanted nothing to do with green chilies. I liked yellow cake with butter-cream frosting and Renata was a chocolate maker's best friend. I loved vibrant bright colors and pastels, and she liked rich dark colors. The fundamental things that we shared were respect for each other and love for our Savior. I entered the food court that day happy and excited to share this time with my friend. We did as opposites do—went to different restaurants and brought our trays to the middle so that we could dine together and talk.

Renata was nervous, and I was hungry. I began to eat as she talked. She began to tell me of an experience that she and her husband had just recently had while attending a marriage counseling session. She talked about some of the exchange, but was very excited to share a spiritual manifestation that was glowing on her and in her. Renata was so encouraged and on fire for how she felt the presence of the Holy Spirit in the gathering. After seven and a half years of marriage, Renata and her husband had began drifting apart. In obedience to her beliefs, she was working on restoring her marriage and renewing their relationship. As I sat and listened to how hopeful she sounded, I was even more excited for what God was going to do for Julius and me. At that moment, I remembered the peace and presence that I received during that October fast. I continued to eat and noticed that Renata had barely touched her food.

She sat up straight in her chair and pursed her lips. Renata is a very expressive talker with her hands going in circular motions like gentle moving ribbons. I watched her movements and stopped eating in anticipation of what was to follow. I looked her square in the eyes as she said, "After, the experience that I just had, I have to be obedient to what I believe God is telling me. And I feel that I cannot be there when you get married." I didn't release her from my gaze, and I looked on in silence and reception. She continued with, "I know that as much as you did for my wedding and how much you were there making it a special day ..." She hesitated and continued, "You are the closest person I have to a sister. I just can't be there. I don't feel that you shouldn't marry Julius. I just think it's not the right time." I was hurt and held my defenses. I allowed her to finish and wrap up her convictions to me. I said what I believed, but it hurt my very core: "I respect your belief. As I told you before, I want the day to be blessed, and if you or anyone else cannot be there and be supportive and happy, then I don't want you there. I understand." I processed her words and on an intellectual level, I respected her and comprehended everything she said. But on that day, my spirit grieved, not with uncertainty of what God had promised me, but the knowledge that my joy was attempting to be stolen. Renata continued to talk and laugh as if everything was normal, as my mind drifted to *what do I do now?*

We finished our lunch—or decided that we weren't going to eat. I instantly lost my appetite, and Renata was still on her spiritual high. We embraced good-bye, as I thought of the need to call the facility to talk to the counselor. As I drove back to work, my heart was racing but my head was empty from my lunch lecture. I asked for the counselor and got her right away. I changed the names on our witness list to Dana and William.

William was a young man I had never met. He was another inmate at the facility with Julius. He was a nice young man who was soon to be released. Julius had liked him and was slightly protective of him. I was going to get married in two weeks, and the only family and friends that would be there did not belong to me yet. That night I prayed for clarity and discernment. The next morning I woke with resolve. What I was experiencing was being stripped of non-necessities and entrusting God with the marriage. I was being molded.

The next two weeks crept by, and my conversing with friends or family almost ceased. I felt alone, but not lonely. I felt like I was Moses going into a foreign land. I did not feel any prophets or prayer warriors around me. I prayed more and listened for God's word to tell me not to marry Julius. I was silent, and God was present. There was not a "no" in my spirit.

As I drove to New York, I found such joy in my solitude. I was happy and at peace, and I knew that God was creating a trophy of grace in this union. I felt His protection, and I also was very familiar with my dependency on Him. Dana followed me in her car on the drive. We arrived at the facility before the eight o'clock requirement. Dana slept in her car as I entered with birth certificate, driver's license, cash and all certainty that I was not alone.

The officer had a list of names for all the soon-to-be-brides and their respective spouses. As we entered the visiting room, the last names were taped to tables to indicate where to sit. There were fourteen women who entered, but fifteen tables with accompanying names. The nervousness was high as women talked between tables. Most of the women were in their early twenties to late thirties, and one woman looked like she was in her mid-fifties to early sixties. After waiting more than a half an hour, the men began to enter sparsely. They smiled as they walked toward their future mates. Julius entered with such nervousness. I smiled as I knew that the next day would finally be our wedding day. There was hand holding and embracing in the room. The counselor walked the room, pacing, as if it were her wedding day. The town clerk, who issues the marriage license had not arrived yet, so it allowed for more time together prior to the licensing procedure. One table over from us and one row back was a young man sitting alone. He fought hard to sit there with dignity in his eyes, as no bride had arrived for him. I did not notice him right away because Julius and I were in our own private gathering.

Julius slid down on one knee and grabbed both of my hands into his. His touch matched mine in intensity and temperature. He looked into my eyes and said, "I love you, sweetness. Will you marry me?" He was talking in a low voice that was above a whisper.

Tears formed in my eyes, but none fell as I said, "Absolutely."

Julius and I talked as we waited our time with the town clerk at a table in the front of the room. When "Whinston" was called, he stood and grabbed my hands to lift me. Julius stared at me the entire time, almost in amazement. I didn't think I looked any different than usual. I wore very little to no makeup. He smiled as he watched me give the town clerk my response to the question of last name: "hyphenate." The process of applying for the license went very quickly, and we were back at our assigned seats in the bliss of each other's company.

The next day would be our big one, and my future husband was more nervous than I had ever seen him. I think I felt a slight tremor in his hold, but his eyes were filled with such assurance that I did not ask if he was afraid. As the last of the couples signed and paid for their license, the single gentleman without a bride walked out of the visiting room. Julius said, "I can only imagine his pain."

The next morning, I woke up and awakened those lazy crickets that awakened the sleeping birds. I was awake before any other creature. I did not sleep much the night before and had showered before 6:00 A.M. I sat on the edge of my bed and prayed as Dana slept. "Thank you, Lord, for your peace that surpasses my understanding. Thank you for blessing me with a man who loves me, protects me, respects me, desires me and believes in me. I thank you for your presence and comfort. I thank you for safe travels. I ask you to bless us this day with your love and joy. Father, make it whole and precious in your sight. In Jesus' name, Amen." I sat for a while in the still of the morning and felt more love than I had known.

Dana finally awoke that morning and drew her bath. She was on the phone most of the morning as I curled my hair and applied makeup. After she exited the bathroom, she began to snap pictures of my preparation. She was going to send them to Julius later.

We were dressed before ten that morning and had lightly eaten from the hotel's continental breakfast. Dana took more pictures both in the hotel lobby and outside as I entered the car. I did feel like a bride on her wedding day. I was full speed ahead to the prison.

We were there more than twenty minutes before our required arrival time of noon. I exited the car and was ready to see my groom. Dana opened her door and asked me to come to the driver's side of the car. She handed me a card and a tiny box. Before I could open either, she said, "Julius wanted me to give this to you before you entered the facility. He asked that you wear it." As I read the card, tears formed in my eyes. I fought them fervently to keep my makeup intact. I was engrossed in his love as I opened the small jewelry box. To my surprise and wonder was a gold necklace with an amulet dangling securely on it. The back was gold and about the size of a dime. In the middle of this circle was a small tan-colored speck seated on the front of a mother pearl face. As I flipped it over, inscribed on the back was MATTHEW 17:20. It read, AMULET OF FAITH. IF YE HAVE FAITH AS A GRAIN OF A MUSTARD SEED … NOTHING SHALL BE IMPOSSIBLE FOR YOU. I could no longer bridle the moisture in my eyes. As I wiped the tears that were streaming down, I said, "He's trying to mess up my makeup." Dana placed the necklace around my neck, and we entered the prison.

I was smiling from the inside out. I think my teeth were sparkling in complement to my rhinestone shoes. We had to pass through the metal detector one at a time. The woman in front of me and her witness had brought the procession to a halt. The witness was rousing the metal detector, and the officer was reciting the rules. The bride smiled a restive one as she turned to her guest who was patting her body down to demonstrate she had nothing concealed.

The metal adjustable hooks from her spaghetti-strapped top were causing the noise. Because she had on only a jacket that matched her skirt, removing the top was not a viable option. The guest made it known, "If I have to remove my top, I will. I'm going to see my friend get married." The officer was annoyed and was not budging on the rules. At this point, there was a building line behind me, and I was certain that a scene was about to be made. Before I could turn back around, the officer's sergeant had released the woman to enter the facility. The officer rebelled with a few words that indicated that he felt his authority had been usurped. His rambling lasted only a few minutes as the remainder of the processional filed through the metal detector. As my turn had come and gone, I wondered what it was like to have a friend committed to be there like that for me.

My marriage to Julius was just moments away. He was one of the last men to walk into the visiting room. He was the tallest and easily identifiable. As each man headed to his table, I stood and watched him walk toward me. He was dressed in a cream dress shirt with a matching cream tie that was one shade darker. From his waist up, he looked like any groom approaching his bride. I focused on his face as he opened his arms to receive me. Julius said, "You look beautiful. Do you like my gift?" I hugged him, and for the first time in a long time I did not kiss him immediately after an embrace. Our next kiss would be him saluting me as his bride. He held me as we moved back toward our seats.

The way Julius beheld me was full of adoration, and I felt our gratitude. It was our time to exchange vows. We stood in the rear of the visiting room. Julius and I were facing each other with Dana to my right and William to Julius' left. The justice of the peace was a merry man possibly in his early sixties. He was respectful and took his time to greet us. He began the ceremony that asked directly if we would take each other as husband and wife. Julius was first, and his reply was "I do." I followed each question with "I will." As I looked into Julius' eyes, with each passing moment, I could see the wetness in the corners. Before any tears fell, the justice of the peace said, "You may kiss your wife." Julius kissed me with enough passion to know that we were married, but with knowledge that people were looking on. He released and grabbed my hand as we walked back to the table.

After the ceremony, he continued to hold my hand and rolled it gently back and forth in his. He was still nervous, but he gave that gorgeous mischievous smile that is usually reserved for rare moments. This time was monumental for us, and it gleamed across his face to the sparkling in his eye. William congratulated us as he joined in the family conversation. Dana was now my sister-in-law, and Julius had made it so in becoming my husband. That day lingered for such a short time, but it was more special than I could have imagined a prison wedding to be. In the twinkling of an eye, the caress of our lips and the stroke of a pen we were married. For the few hours that we were given, we created or own reception, and it was delightful.

The visit and weddings were called to an end some two-plus hours later. We stood and embraced. I was to visit the following day, so it wouldn't be the lengthy breaks that we usually experienced. However, as he released me and stepped back, I knew that the usual couple departure in limos or horse-drawn carriages was not to follow. Surprisingly, I did not feel melancholic. Instead I said, "I'll see you tomorrow, Mr. Whinston." He followed my cue and said, "I'll see you, too, Mrs. Whinston."

Dana and I left the facility and drove back to the hotel. When I opened the door to our room, there were red roses for me on the desk. I read the card: ON YOUR WEDDING DAY. WELCOME TO THE FAMILY. LOVE, DANA, TOYA AND CHRIS. Dana had arranged for me to have fresh, beautiful red roses on our wedding day. I was so grateful for her kindness and her desire to make the day special for me. She treated me to dinner before she departed to drive back to Cleveland.

When I returned to the room after the long day, I was extremely tired. I washed my face and made a few phone calls. I called my bible study friends to thank them for their prayers. Each one was excited with me over the miles. I had one in Atlanta, another in Dayton and the last one in Tallahassee. I called Simone to check on Quincy, and I reveled in the stories of what my new sister-in-law had done. The last call I made was to Myeisha. She was not happy for me, and in her dissatisfaction she turned to humor. There were no congratulations or best wishes. Myeisha said, "Well at least your last name isn't Willis." Mentioning Quincy's last name was meant to be a slap in the face. I told her it was not funny, and I hung up the phone. In spite of her wicked and cruel joke, I was not saddened or discouraged. I turned on the television and climbed into bed. I imagined Julius there as I fell asleep.

The next day, I visited the facility, and for the first time I wrote "wife" in the area that asked for relationship. For the past three years, it was written in as "friend." Julius and I were now best friends, and he was my husband. We visited the remainder of that day in laughter and celebration.

Julius wrote me even more often after we were married. It was like we had a role reversal. He became more sensitive and made sure that I knew how special and valued I was to him. I in turn wanted him to know how desired and wanted he was by me. Our letters went back and forth for months, just addressing each other in our new roles.

Around August, we were facing Julius' second parole appearance. We took our time compiling his parole package and increased information on future plans, resources and support mechanisms for him upon his release. We had letters from governmental agencies, support groups and other organizations and people willing to make his integration back into society a reliable success. The mounting anxiety did not cause us to squabble this time around. Julius and I kept working or putting together the best parole package that we both would be proud of.

That August we planned a family visit with Dana, Toya, Chris and Stephanie, Julius' youngest daughter. That weekend had been authorized for such a special visit. We would spend Saturday and Sunday together as a family. We played cards and just spent time talking. The visit was intended to take Julius' mind off the upcoming board and provide him needed encouragement. The visit did not go completely as planned, but it did end with a group prayer for his board appearance.

I was as prepared as I could be when I called the facility to talk to the parole counselor to hear the decision. Mr. Lawson went through a series of questions to ensure that I was indeed Julius' wife and privy to the disclosure of the board. He said, "He has twenty-four more months." I didn't fall apart or even cry. I was a pillar of experience and grounded in faith. Mr. Lawson continued with, "He will have in writing exactly what the board says as to their reasoning." I thanked him and hung up. Two days later, I received Julius' letter. We both were emotionally different this parole hearing, but nonetheless relenting on working for his eventual release. Our fight was unified.

Time was just dragging by. There was no big event for us to focus on. The wedding had come and gone, and the second parole appearance had as well. We had our mountain high the day we wed and not quite a valley low with the second parole denial. We needed something else to work toward. We were maintaining well, but Julius was looking for another transfer.

This move was going to be highly unlikely. Julius had only been at this present facility for under a year. He had no downgrade of his classification or programming that would require him to transfer anywhere. He was stuck and hating the facility he was in. We both had written letters and exhausted every avenue for him to leave. We were going to have to wait another year, and then hope when he transferred he was not farther away. Things were just stagnant. We were still in love and committed to each other, and we were 370 miles apart. Julius was unable to get any more trade programs as deemed by the department of corrections that he had been given sufficient amount of programs, so he worked the mess hall, and we continued to write. It seemed that most doors for change were closed for us.

God's favor can open windows that are unavailable to many. At the beginning of December, Julius was transferred at the request of someone who had enough authority to make the decision happen almost immediately. Within ten days, Julius was being transferred again. I had always been pretty non-emotional about his relocations. I was simply "give me the facts" or "if it gets you better situated to come home, then we can make the sacrifice." This next move was a blessing in more ways the one. I celebrated Christmas on December 9 when I learned Julius was going to the closest facility in New York to Ohio. Our distance was now 309 miles, and the new facility allowed for family reunion visits (FRP). I still desperately wanted him home, but I craved time alone with him right then. We would have to wait thirty days after his transfer before we could apply for the family reunion program.

I was re-energized, and although Julius tried to hide it, he was too. By the middle of January, we were waiting for an approval for our first FRP. If approved, we would have forty-four hours together in an apartment-type setting that allowed us to cook, eat, sleep and be intimate with each other. This wait seemed longer than the five-month delay in our wedding date. I swear, I was looking at the calendar, putting everything on a timetable. By February, we had a spring date for exactly eleven months and one day after we wed. Julius really preferred to have our first anniversary together, but my impatience and desire to be with my husband won out.

I was planning a weekend getaway with Julius, and I was ecstatic. I was so excited that I was driving anyone and everyone who knew nuts. I was counting down, shopping, packing and revising my travel plans. By the week before my departure, I was no longer sleeping through the night. My anticipation was waking me at three or four o'clock in the morning. Julius and I were going to make this a honeymoon and anniversary all rolled into one. Initially, I wanted to make all these plans for all the things I wanted to do with him within the confines of being on state property. Instead, he took charge and wanted to make it a relaxing and pampering day for me. Julius had every intention to take care of me, and I was prepared to let him do just that.

On my arrival date, I had a letter that Julius requested that I open in the parking lot before I entered the facility. He had created a game for us to play. The game was very simple, and he had three indicators of gesturing with my finger to signify what I wanted and the answer had to always be "yes." I was more than game and up to the challenge. If he was asking for anything, "yes" would not be a problem.

I dressed up for our first visit. I wore a suit with dress sandals and a matching blouse. It was a special date for us. In New York, it was raining and cold, but I didn't care. I tiptoed through puddles trying to keep my toes dry and warm. After loading the van with clothes and food for the weekend, we took a short ride to a secluded area of the facility reserved for such family visits. As the van approached, I noticed the row type of units similar to apartments. I saw Julius come off the deck area to meet the van. The officer opened the door, and it took everything in me not to jump right into Julius' arms. Julius helped me step out of the van and grabbed my things. I stood there just for a moment so he could kiss me in the rain and in the open. We walked into the dwelling, and he had cleaned and organized his things. The place had the aroma of his cologne. It was dark, but not without light. The appearance was similar to the lighting at dawn.

I removed my shoes as I entered, and we stood in the open kitchen and dining area. I grabbed him, and he moved into my arms. I was smiling and kissing him. He was rubbing my back, and in my mind I was already undressed. Julius was holding me so tight, and I was yielding to his embrace. I was trying to prepare myself for the game he had created for us, although I was wondering what game.

As we stood in the kitchen for those first few moments, I felt a sense of home in him that I had never experienced. I walked to him and he moved backward into the hallway. We sauntered into the bedroom and stood in the doorway. As he slid his hands around my waist and up the back of my blouse, I stared at him in admiration. I was saying, "Yes, I will" as I stroked the outside of his arm. I had every intention to open myself up to Julius so that he might enter the inner courts of me. We were swaying to the unevenness of our statures and the unfamiliarity of our stances. I removed my slacks and stood as close to Julius as I could. We were pursuing each other in that moment. It was coming out of non-recognition into knowingness.

I lifted my arms above my head and to the side of his face. I stroked him both gently and soothingly. I was there to meet his need in the emotional and physical immediacy. I intended to be the Proverbs 18:22 wife. "The man who finds a wife finds a treasure and receives favor from the LORD." (NLT) I massaged and stroked his head from the top and along the back. I relinquished myself into his command. He untied my blouse and slowly unwrapped into a fully accessible opening. Every wall and barrier was coming down.

Julius stood there for a moment before removing another item of my clothing. He was fully dressed, and I was being presented to him in the quietness and sanctity of that room. I breathed him, and in my heart I desired to be a Proverbs 31 wife. Julius was to have everything, and in this moment he was going to know living in his privilege. I wanted to be worth more than rubies. And I felt the satin feel of his hands remove the remaining garments. I kissed and acknowledged his slightest touch. I wanted his full attention and confidence. I was there to heal open and aching wounds of abandonment. I touched him with all the goodness I felt for him, and I cloaked him in the protectiveness of my love. Julius moved me and guided me to our wedding bed. I closed my eyes as I dreamed of far-away places still wrapped in his arms. I wanted him to emotionally dine on me. It was exotic, embarking on paradise. I was determined for him to have no limits to his territories or boundaries. I held him and pulled him into me as we traveled over the surface of the cotton sheets. He was still fully clothed as he took liberties customary for a spouse. I was leading and following at the same time. I touched his hands in affirmation, advancing him to places I wanted him to know. He obliged and catenated every location that I had preceded his next movement. I opened the vineyard, and he drank of me. I watched over his every need, and he fed mine. In those early hours of that day and long into the late hours of that afternoon, we discovered newness in each other. I had "I will" on my tongue and in my heart.

As we lay in the stillness of the night, I quietly recited my written vows to him.

I promise to love you faithfully and honestly for as long as God gives us breath.

… to join this union with a joyful spirit and a committed heart

… to support and respect you as the head of our family and to nurture and edify you as my life partner and friend

... to accept our children as blessings from God and guide them so that they may be productive, complete and loving people

... to be a fertile haven for your mind, body and spirit and to be open to receive the same in return

... to endow our goals and dreams and continue to work toward them until they come to pass

... to celebrate and rejoice with you in good times and to encourage and stand firm beside you in bad

... to have pride, be submissive and humble myself so that forgiveness is always welcome

... to serve you without reservation and accept the same in return

... to cherish you as a continuous gift from God.

I was thanking God for Julius in this occasion and remembering the journey we had chosen. We had taken a leap of faith that still had a narrative yet to unfold. I was lulling in the warmth of his embrace and cradled in the certainty that "nothing shall be impossible for us."

"Grief is a profound part of recovery and new life.

Tears of regret, remorse and despair water the roots of love and life itself.

To deny and avoid the hurts and pains of life is to negate life's importance …"

—*Author Unknown*

Life sure has a way of making you face the things in your life that you've swept under the rug. Terry's love for me was so wonderful, so awesome and over-whelming. He made me happy but then life came crashing down on me. Share my journey with me. Come and walk with me.

—*Rayna*

Come and Walk with Me

Rhonda L. Harris

My life seemed wonderful. It felt like I had it all—the man, the career and the family. I was married to the man of my dreams, even though he was in prison. My extended family had finally accepted the fact that Terry wasn't going anywhere and that he would continue to be a very big part of my life. The next few years of our lives were really blissful. We were madly in love. We had the support of our family and friends. We were very happy. Everything seemed perfect, and I was determined to keep it that way.

I have always been a very independent woman—a control freak even. When I married Terry, I was forced to step up my game even further. Now I had one more piece of the puzzle to juggle. I had so many balls up in the air and wouldn't dare to let any of them fall. I became a Superwoman. I worked all day, studied public policy all evening, wrote love letters at midnight and made weekend trips to the prison to see Terry.

Living the life of being a prison wife ain't no joke. No one told me that in this life you always have to fight. You have to fight to sustain your relationship. You are always trying to validate it for someone. You always have to defend your relationship—and your man—to your family and to your friends. You have to fight to protect the good man that you love while shielding his crime, his past, from the inquiring minds who all want to know what he did.

There is so much negativity, so many stereotypes and stigmas associated with being an inmate's wife. I know that because of all of the family and societal disapproval around me that I worked even harder to make sure that our family unit remained intact. We were not going to be another statistic. We would not contribute to the number of failed prison marriages or to the number of failed black marriages period. My obsession with overcoming the shortsightedness of others drove me to the point of self-destruction.

I took care of everything. I took care of our girls, which involved rising with the birds to get them to school and me to work on time. Our evenings were full of the usual stuff like homework, dinner, playtime, bath time, story time and then bedtime. I studied most nights until eleven, then I would spend an hour or so writing to Terry. I took care of Terry too. His family had given him a little support during his time but not nearly enough. I had to make sure he had everything he needed and most of what he wanted, even though he never asked. I worked in this crazy unit at the bank. We were a mandatory overtime environment. Even though I was the supervisor, I worked just as hard and as long as my staff. I couldn't leave them there with hours of work left to be done and be content to be sitting at home chilling. I took care of the bills, including our three-hundred-dollar-a-month telephone bill. I continued running at this pace for almost five years. I really thought I had everything all under control. I only wish that were the case. I was on autopilot—I just did it all. But I felt so empty, so lost. The reality was that I took care of everything and everyone but me then gradually it started to rain. Abruptly then the thundering began. The rumbling inside of my head was deafening. The weight upon my chest grew heavier each day. It all grew faster and more intense with each passing day. What was wrong with me? I wondered. I prayed for some insight into this phase of life into which I seemed thrust. I had lots of questions but very few answers.

I focused on my symptoms: headaches, tension, stress and anxiety. I took every over-the-counter pill I could find to try to ease these feelings. This was my daily existence as I suffered. Nothing I did, nothing I took made me feel any better. Nothing would relieve this agony. When I couldn't take it any longer I went to see my doctor.

The first question my doctor asked me after I described my symptoms was "What has changed in your life since I saw you last year?" I replied, "This is what's new, Dr. Douglass:

- I have a new job that I love but I'm working seventy-plus hours a week.

- I'm tired all of the time.

- I'm salaried on the new job so all of that overtime that I use to depend on is gone.

- I'm struggling to make ends meet.

- My car is about to be repossessed.

- I'm on the verge of filing bankruptcy.

- I'm emotionally drained.

- My emotional eating is out of control—see how much weight I've gained?

- And lastly, I've married a man in prison who is serving life."

I have never heard Dr. Douglass laugh in the four years that he has been treating me, but he looked me straight in the eye and chuckled when he said, "Well, it's easy to see why you're having anxiety attacks and migraines." My aunt Bea would always talk about her migraines but I never knew what they were, how they felt or even how they were different from a headache. But now I knew. Dr. Douglass suggested that I make an appointment with a psychologist to talk through some of this stuff that I was going through to help me release some of this tension. He feared that if I didn't get help that I would eventually have a nervous breakdown. "Not me," I said to him. "I have a degree in psychology. I'm the counselor to my family and friends. I don't need counseling. Besides, don't you think that I would know if I needed help?" I was adamant about believing that I was going to be just fine. I left his office thinking that he was crazy, but I also left with a prescription for the migraines, and I headed back to work. *I'm going to be okay,* I thought.

It suddenly dawned on me that the pressure weighing against my chest grew heavier as Fridays neared. My weekly journey "over the river and through the woods" to Terry's house was becoming a chore. I now dreaded the drive I used to love so much. The snowcapped mountaintops were no longer beautiful to me. I knew that I couldn't keep up this pace much longer.

Something had to give. I just prayed that it wouldn't be me. "Please, God, don't let anything happen to me. They all need me, they're all counting on me. Don't take me now" became my daily mantra. I still had not revealed any of what I was going through to Terry. I had to live up to the image of a strong black woman (SBW) that he professed me to be and that I lived up to being. Everything around me revolved around me. Without me, nothing happened, I believed. I knew I needed some help but I wouldn't dare ask for it. I was a SBW and everyone depended on me to simply keep it moving, so that's exactly what I did.

One night while I was writing in my journal I had ideas of love, and the question of how I love me was at the forefront of my mind. I wrote: I love Terry with all of my heart. I cherish our family. But how do I love me? How am I loving me? I knew that these thoughts came forth for a reason but life had to keep moving. I couldn't stop and take the time to explore that at the moment. The girls and I were leaving the next morning for our family visit. That evening, while the girls were asleep, I revisited the thoughts of the night before. I knew that I wasn't taking care of me like I should. I wondered how to fix this, how to fix me. I didn't know what to do. As I prayed, I began to meditate on the words of Oleta Adam's song "Come and Walk with Me." The song tells the story of a soul feeling beaten down and alone but just when things were the darkest that soul called upon God and He walked her to the other side—that other side where one is spiritually free. As I drifted off to sleep, I had peace. I didn't have a clear answer on what to do next, but I knew that it was time for me to get out of my own way and let the Father take over. I knew that everything would be okay—that I would be okay.

The girls and I were the first family to arrive at the facility the next morning. I was so looking forward to our family visit this time, not so much because Terry and I would be able to share our intimate times but because his being there would give me a break from being "on" 24/7. Terry would be there to entertain and occupy the girls, and I could get some much-needed rest and relaxation.

The more I thought about the idea of taking a break, the better it sounded, and the more relaxed and relieved I became. Just the thought of getting away from this madness was a stress reliever. All five families having family visits that day piled into the van, and we bumped along the snow-covered road from the main gate to the trailers. I couldn't stop staring at the mountaintops. They were beautiful to me again. I felt at ease. This moment was surreal.

Terry and the other husbands were waiting at the gate for the van to pull up so they could unload all of our stuff for our weekend getaway. Terry grabbed most of the bags.The girls dragged their suitcases to the trailer. They were so cute out there in their snowsuits trying to help Daddy with the bags. I love my family. I love Terry with all of my heart. As I watched him, I was simply in awe. He is truly the best thing to happen to me and the girls, yet I knew that it was my time to take a break.

Terry and I made passionate love while the girls took their nap. I got out of bed to shower while Terry just laid there, I presume basking in the afterglow. I turned around and stopped dead in my tracks in the doorway, looked into his eyes and then down at the floor. I didn't want to see his face as I uttered the words, "I can't do this anymore."

Terry jumped out of bed, grabbed my hand and led me to the bed to sit next to him. He said, "Baby, talk to me." I cried as I told him all of the things I had been keeping from him. I told him about my ever-growing debt, the physical exhaustion from working so many long hours, my total lack of energy, how the twelve-hour drive to and from his place was beginning to take its toll on me and on the car, the warring inside of my head and the strain against my chest.

He became sad, and the tears began to fall from his eyes, but at that moment of his extreme sorrow, my mood instantly changed from one of sadness to serenity. I had told Terry everything. I had released it all to him and out into the universe. I was free. I was beginning to take control of my fate instead of being an innocent bystander merely going with the flow. He asked me if I was leaving him, if I wanted a divorce. I cried as I told him no. I told him that when we married I made a promise to him and to God that our marriage would end only when death us did part. I told him that I just needed to take some time for me to figure out what I was doing, where I was going and to straighten some things out in my head. I tried to assure Terry that this was not about him, but it was entirely all about me.

Terry's next remark and his mood is one that I will never forget. In a tone I had never heard Terry use in the five years that we had been together, he said to me, "Hell no. You ain't taking no break from me." I have to admit that his tone did take me aback. I saw a side of Terry that I had not seen before. He was scared. My first response was to just go off. I thought, *He knows that my mouth is set on springs, that all I need is a trigger and my mouth can discharge some hurtful things on a moment's notice, so why would he even want to go there with me?* Who does he think he is to tell me what I am and what I'm not going to do?

I restrained my tongue and simply reminded Terry of his promise to me the day before we wed. It had been a sunny November day. I got to the facility bright and early to complete our premarital paperwork. Afterward we had a very serious conversation. Terry said to me that if ever there came a time when I felt like this life of being an inmate's wife was too much for me and I needed a break to just say so and we'd work through it. He promised to always be supportive and patient with me when and if that time ever came. I asked him if he recalled saying those words to me on the eve of our wedding. He didn't answer me; he just sat there in silence looking down at the floor. After a few minutes he said, "I love you, Rayna."

I softly said, "I love you, too, Terry."

We didn't speak of my taking a break during the rest of the visit, though we both knew that this wouldn't be the last time we would speak on the subject. The next time we made love, it was the same, yet it was different; we were the same; yet we were different—everything was different.

The drive home felt longer this time. I kept replaying the weekend in my head. I knew that I had to take care of me. I knew that this was best for us all. I wondered if and when Terry would realize that it was the best for us too. I felt awful. I only wanted to bring Terry love and happiness. I never wanted to cause him any pain. He had experienced his share of pain in his life through his own circumstance. I was to be that bright light for him. The girls were the apples of his eye. But I was causing the man I love heartache and grief. Terry was saddened terribly by my needing to take a break from the life of being a prison wife.

All I kept thinking about was Terry's phone call, which would come the moment I walked in the house. We had the timing down to a science. Terry knew when we should arrive home, and he always called like clockwork to make sure we made it safely. I wasn't sure what I would say. I wondered what he'd say. I felt miserable because I felt like a part of me was dying. I also felt like a part of us was dying. As much as it hurt, I knew that this break couldn't be avoided and it had to happen. The phone rang the moment I turned the key in the door. The first thing Terry said was that he loved me. I told him that I loved him too. I tried to explain to him that because I loved him so much that I needed to take some time to love me, fix the things in me that weren't right.

Terry went on giving me all of these compliments like, "Baby, you are perfect to me … you're wonderful … nothing about you needs fixing." And it was really starting to piss me off because he was listening but he wasn't hearing me. Instead he kept saying things that I didn't need to hear or even want to hear. I tried to be understanding because I knew that he was holding on by a thread. I knew that the girls and I were the only glimmer of happiness that he had seen in the eighteen years he had been down. I knew that we were all he had. We were his family—his life. I know that he felt like he was losing everything. Besides what could Terry really do to help me through this? He was locked up—not here. I had to do this all alone. I was even angry with him because he wasn't there. I know that may sound crazy because I met him inside and he had never been out with me, but that didn't make me need him here any less. Even though I knew all of these things, I had to put what Terry wanted out of my head in order to stay focused on healing me.

Was I being heartless? Selfish? Cruel? Maybe so, but I knew that I had to do what was best for me. I prayed that in time Terry would realize that it was also best for him and for us. I had to distance myself a bit from Terry and the situation in order to not let love cloud my thoughts and more importantly my judgment. I decided that it would be best for us not to talk for a while, at least until I was able to sort out all of the junk that I needed to work on. I asked him not to call. I told him not to put in a new application for a trailer visit. I told him that we would just write for a while. I tried to reassure him that I was not leaving him, yet everything I said felt like I was. We both cried as we said good-bye.

I called in sick to work the next two days. I needed some time. I don't know what made me think that after two days that everything would be fine, but I persevered. During my hiatus, I didn't sleep much if at all. I wrote down all of the things in my life that needed shifting. My list seemed to be continuously growing. The short list ended up looking a lot like this:

- Spiritual: I need help in my spiritual walk. I feel like I am losing faith in God, in myself, in everything.

- I am beginning to struggle with Terry and I not being aligned spiritually. It really feels like I'm doing battle all alone.

- Physical: I'm overweight still. My migraines continue and my blood pressure is still on the rise.

- Mental: There are so many issues from my childhood that still continue to plague me.

- Financial: I am damn near broke.

As I wrote out this list I realized that my deciding to take a break from Terry had nothing really to do with Terry, but all of my issues affected how I was with Terry. Hell, I was a mess. I knew that in order to be any good to Terry and the girls, I had to get myself together. The pity party was over. It was time for change.

This journey from the darkness into the light was a long and arduous one for us both. My forcing this break on Terry actually ignited his own personal journey of redefining himself. He was a wonderful black man whose true potential remained untapped. I prayed daily that his strength never failed him. He was bright, educated and strong, yet extremely frustrated. He was tired of being inside. He had spent more years inside than he had on the outside. His frustration came from being locked in a world whose primary goal was to keep him down. He was in a constant battle with himself not to succumb from the madness inside. He struggled with his fellow inmates to try to keep them out of trouble. He was always called on to help fix this and that or bail someone out of something. His control was constantly challenged by COs whose dick got hard when they wielded their façade of control, trying to make him snap. He also had to fend off the voices of his own boys inside who told him that I was crazy, "on some shit," unfaithful, disloyal, not to be trusted and just about every other negative truism they could think of to try to assassinate my character. My Terry was stuck in a world of misery loves company personified.

I had a lot of hard work to do, too, to resolve all of my issues and be able to return to love for myself, for Terry and for us. But I was ready to do the work. I took my list of issues and began working through them. I started first and foremost with my spiritual life. Even though I faithfully attended church on Sunday, I rarely picked up the Word after I left the sanctuary. I began an intense bible study and read a number of spiritual books. I needed to feel that my faith and strength were unwavering. I needed to know that I could survive this and any other adversity that came along. The more I read, I saw more areas where I needed work. The revelations were painful and beneficial all the same.

I knew that I had to shatter my strongholds and work through them in order to free my spirit of them. I never realized how much power and control I had allowed my pain and insecurities to have over my life. I realized that my insecurities obtained life early on in my childhood.

From as far back as I can remember, I always felt as though I was never good enough. I felt that the house we lived in, the neighborhood we lived in and the lack of money measured up to me never being good enough. I remember when I was about eight years old, I vowed that my mother's life would not be mine. I was determined to not be a member of the poor working class in black America. I knew then that my only way out was through education. I started to read everything I could get my hands on—from the ingredients on the cereal box to *National Geographic*. I would beg my mom to take me to the library every Saturday so I could just sit there for hours, reading and even taking notes. I would just go to a shelf and grab any book that for some reason caught my eye. It seemed like the more I learned, the sadder my mother became.

I remember being in the third grade in a split 3rd and 4th grade class. I would be so bored with my work that I would do the fourth graders' work too. When my teacher noticed this, she called for a meeting with my mom and the guidance counselor at my school, requesting that I be moved up to the fourth grade. I was thrilled. I felt like I was well on my way to being good enough. I didn't have money but I had brains, and I was ready for success, even then. When Mom said no, I was heated. Why would she want to hold me back? Why was she trying to keep me down? Why did she want me to end up like her? The anger and resentment began to build.

My stepfather, Eddie, called me Sapphire when I was little. I used to think that it was because I was born in September, but right after my mother refused to let me be skipped, he explained to me the history of the persona of Sapphire and why I reminded him of her. Sapphire was a character played by Ernestine Wade on the *Amos and Andy* television show.

She was stout, medium to dark brown, headstrong and opinionated. Yes, I was all of those things, even as I child. Even though Eddie was no match for Mom when her mind was made up, he always encouraged me to keep excelling and in due season my time to shine would come. Eddie was right. The following school year, unbeknownst to me, my fifth-grade teacher Mrs. Bath submitted my name for acceptance into City Honors, the honors school in our town. I was so excited when she informed me and my mom that I had been accepted. I was on my way to being good enough despite my mother's efforts to keep me back. I was still holding on to that resentment, and it was eating away at me. I kept ignoring it though. All I focused on was my studies and counting down the days until I would be grown and could move into my own place and be my own woman.

I graduated from high school with honors and moved into my own place. I was in college full time, working full time, driving my first car, and I had my own apartment. I had it going on. The day I met Darnell, the girls' father, was the best and worst day of my life. I was so infatuated with this fine black man. I overlooked all of his bad traits just to gaze at his beautiful face. When everybody saw him, they remarked on how much he looked like actor Will Smith. Darnell resembles him in looks and build, and he even has that boyish grin and Hollywood charm. The worst part about Darnell is that he knew it. Yes, he was cute. All of the girls thought he was fine. Most women would probably drop at his feet. The worst part was that he didn't like women as such as he loved himself. I knew it, too, yet I stayed. I thought that being with someone like him—no, let me correct that, being with someone who looked like him made me look good, good enough.

Darnell was the perfect man while in my sight, but when I was away he always played. He was truly a serial polygamist. Our relationship and marriage was intense, passionate and furious, all wrapped up into one. We yelled, screamed, cursed, broke things and then would have the best makeup sex known to man. Trina was actually conceived during one of our makeup sexcapades. My life with Darnell was an episode of temporary insanity that went on for five years. Although he was a poor excuse for a husband—hell, even a man—he blessed me with my two daughters, and for that I will always be thankful. Don't get me wrong. I never want to see him get run over by a truck or anything, but if I ever saw him again in life, it would be too soon. I love him being the check-in-the-mail father.

I had to just let it all go—the childhood issues and those insecurity issues. They were this black cloud that loomed over me and kept me from fully appreciating Terry's ray of sunshine that sparkled in my life. Over the next few months, I shared all of these things with Terry, plus so much more in my many marathon letters to him. This process of cleansing my spirit of such negativity was an educational one for Terry. Through sharing all of my stuff with him, he gained a better and deeper understanding of me. Terry responded by doing the same. The best part of our break was that it allowed us time for mutual and continual growth of ourselves and of our relationship because through each interaction we learned so much more about each other.

Our meeting each other behind the wall allowed us to get to know each other in all of the most important areas of life and love, but we were missing so many of the details. It is the details of our lives that has shaped us into the people we are and the people we'd become. Truth be told, there are only so many details that can be transcribed in letters, spoken during a thirty-minute telephone call or shared on a six-hour visit. I would advise anyone who meets their love behind the wall to focus on the details too.

Now it was time to focus on how Terry and I would and could align ourselves spiritually when we practiced two different faiths. What was he to do? What was I do? We had promised to never pressure the other to convert. Although Terry and I never talked much about spirituality in the beginning of our relationship, we both knew that all of the answers lay in our faith in God. We knew that we came together because of His divine intervention. God alone gave us the opportunity and ability to love each other fully within this world of oppression. We both held fast to the belief that what God has joined together let no man put asunder—including ourselves. We learned to come together, not in religion, but in faith. Terry remained a Muslim and I remained a Christian. We both put God first in our individual lives, yet He seemed to be absent from our marriage. We began to pray collectively for His guidance in our marriage. Even though our practices were different, keeping God first and always referring to His Word helped us to further solidify the foundation we had built.

Now, it was time to come home. The day we returned to love was a beautiful one in May. Out of the blue Terry called me even though the rule was not to. In an instant I felt my spirit become renewed. "I am ready, I am whole and I am healed. Terry, I need you. I need you to love me like only you can. I need you to take care of me in the special way that you do and never let me go," I said. He so eloquently said, "I will." Spiritually, we renewed our vows and have never looked back. On that day, the clouds separated and the sun began to shine. As I lay in bed that night, I thought about love and I wrote in my journal, "I love Terry, I love us, and I love me."

As I sit here writing today some seven years after our struggle, I am thankful for all of the experiences that I have had with Terry. His love, patience and devotion have helped me become the woman, wife and mother that I am. Reflecting on our love and life is one of my favorite things to do. Loving him, us and me has been a wonderful journey. When I recall the first notion of love for Terry, I think back to the day he touched my hand. Of course I thought he was fine and wished he was mine, but it was something more than that. It was like I could see into his soul. I could feel his spirit. I could see that he was a good man, destined to become a great man. I felt love in my heart when I read his written words on the many early letters that swept me off my feet. I felt love and those butterflies in my stomach whenever we talked on the phone. When we had our first date, I felt love when he kissed my cheek. I felt love between my thighs the day before we married when he kissed me good-bye and caressed my breasts. The day we consummated our marriage, I felt love in the way he touched me so passionately, so tenderly, in the ways our bodies automatically moved in unison, rhythmically, methodically, as though our souls were meant to croon together forever.

When did I fall in love with us? Each and every time I think about Terry and our union, I fall in love with us. I see a strong, beautiful black woman who is madly in love with a strong, beautiful black man. Terry is a man who has shown me nothing but unconditional love, care, concern, passion, sensitivity and strength. I strive to live by his example. Terry is the perfect head of our family. He is the leader. His depth of spirituality always gives me the strength, guidance and protection that I need. From him I have learned the true meanings of faithfulness and perseverance in good times and in bad. I don't want to trivialize the agony that we both endured during our time of struggle, yet we persevered.

I love our compatibility, our connectedness, our open and honest communication, camaraderie, spirituality and passion. Most of all, I love how we fit together. Michelle McKinnney Hammond's words in *Secrets of an Irresistible Woman* describes us to a tee: "I know that I was created from some man's rib. When we encounter each other, he won't be able to help himself because I'm his missing piece. He will be able to accommodate all that I am because I will be the extension of all that he is." Rejoice with me because, in the end, I came home. I came home to me. I am now armed to do battle not just for my husband, but for myself. I came home to the man who prayed for my protection during my years of internal struggle. I came home to the man who has always been my covering through our good times and bad. I came home to love—love of me, love of us and love of him.

Terry is my life. I am with him for the duration, inside or outside of those prison walls. He is my reality for the rest of my life, even if that life means an eternity of trailer visits, regular visits and long-distance phone calls. Naturally, every day I pray that we will enjoy life out here home together someday soon, but if it never happens, it really doesn't matter because we are together and we are love.

When I think about the love that he has shown me, the love he possesses for me, how good he makes me feel when I read his written words and hear his voice, I am often overwhelmed by how good I feel in his presence. No one has ever made me feel like this. He knows that my love for him has no end. He knows that there may be times when I need him to be my solider. I hear ya, Beyonce. I need him to be on guard for me—to catch me and protect me. He is always there and always ready. Terry is fully equipped. He was born to fight. He has had to fight his way through the penal system, fight for his own survival inside and fight for the love of a lifetime. Terry rose to the occasion and to the challenge of loving me.

Today, one God is the source of our faith and the foundation of our marriage. We have learned how to share our prayers, hopes, dreams and especially our doubts and fears. Our Father revealed His magnificence as we traveled on this journey. He helped us to heal us. He walked with Terry, He walked with us, and He walked with me. I know that I am good enough, worthy and blessed. Terry loves me, I love Terry, I love us, and I love me.

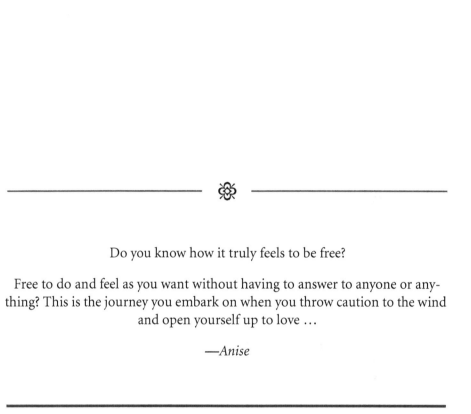

Do you know how it truly feels to be free?

Free to do and feel as you want without having to answer to anyone or anything? This is the journey you embark on when you throw caution to the wind and open yourself up to love ...

—*Anise*

To Love

Susan Goins-Castro

"And now abide faith, hope, love, these three; but the greatest of these is love."

—*1 Corinthians 13:13*

Feel me, feel my desire for I am the essence of love.

Out of all human passions, love is the strongest of them all.

It attacks you simultaneously through your head, your heart and your soul.

It ignites a flow of passion that stimulates your senses in a way to which nothing is comparable.

Love's presence is serene, peaceful and calming. It surrounds and embraces you.

It makes you feel as though you are suspended in time.

It renders you powerless when it captures you while making you feel invincible to the world.

It's a bright beam of light, dancing in the moonlight.

This is how it feels to love …

I sojourned, then I dwelt, now I abide. Julius had captured my heart and rendered me motionless. I visited him for what was intended to be temporary. As I experienced him, I began to long for a dwelling. The journey was opening new adventures to me. I was a weary traveler who found her home. His love gave me pause, and I surrendered to its power, which ignited my passion, calmed my fears and passionately embraced me.

I was dancing in the beam of light because his love is neutralizing.

—*Naomi*

His Love Is Neutralizing

R.Y. Willingham

"I'm in love," I said, and it felt so good. There's no other euphoric emotion that has ever competed equally with such ferociousness. It can override a stressful day with bright thoughts of that special someone. Julius was my special someone, and he woke me every morning and stroked my hair every night. That sounds crazy, but in my heart and in my mind, it was true. And I held him close.

Just as the madness of him being with me was my daily dose of soulful healing, I had desires of him that surpassed any physical memory that we shared. I was almost ready to say "yes" to any question he asked. Julius knew, and that made it all more alluring.

I still visited him heavily in the summer with our dates trailing off just as the temperature declined. During one of those hot months, we chose to have our visit outside under a small pavilion. The picnic tables were spread more sparsely apart, and the sunshine and warm breeze allowed us to transcend the razor wire to what felt much like a date in the park. Certainly if we glanced behind us and lifted our heads high we could see the officer seated in the tower above us keeping his security watch. Nonetheless, we erased his presence and courted each other in the most awkward courtyard I had ever seen. Julius held my warm hand in his coolness. Over many visits, I realized that just as opposites attract, his touch felt cold and mine eagerly complemented his with my heat. It was warmth that could easily go from a comfortable sixty-five degrees straight to 101 in the shade after sufficient hand holding, a kiss engaged too long and hearing his voice say, "Sweetness." We laughed and talked as hours rolled by on the six-hour weekly visitation clock.

We would break from our laughter and playfulness to partake in the vending machine smorgasbords. It allowed us to stretch our legs and walk a short distance in each other's embrace.

I loved that part. I adored Julius' touch. His caress reminded me that my skin has millions of neurons that were susceptible to the slightest sensation. And when Julius touched me, I swear sometimes my mind got more confused because my mouth watered with loose, warm, free saliva that was balanced in volume by the wetness between my thighs. I ached for him, and he pacified it with firm holding of my hand and gentle caresses of my arm. I was for real crazy. I could have an orgasm that would lift me slightly above my seat while I leaned into his kiss, forcing restricted desire against the softness of his lips. It's enough to make any woman crazy, and again I was almost ready to say, "Yes, oh hell yes" to any question he asked.

In the back of my mind I heard him say, "Sweetness, open up for me." I swear I heard it. My heart was racing so rapidly that you could visibly see the vein in my neck pulsating, trying to force any horse out of the gate. I kissed harder and held him longer. He departed from me with just enough space for air and his question.

"Will you marry me?" he asked.

"Huh?" was my schoolgirl reply.

In the intoxication of his embrace I fought for my sobriety to hear the words come out of his mouth. Julius did not ask again, but he smoothly pushed back slightly in his seat so he could see the fullness of my face and meet me eye-to-eye. I was stunned. It was not because I was surprised by his question, but it was like asking me to get a drink of water while gorging on some splendid champagne. I did not respond. I had learned in this short time that honesty would be paramount in our relationship. There would be no little lies—those white ones or shades of yellow—nor would there be deception and dishonesty in who we were. I quietly rocked myself back to a secure place on that park bench, and said, "Not now." I did not back it up with explanation or excuses or belabored defense. I did not cop out. I said, "Not now." That's an apprehensive way of saying, "I may say yes."

Julius surprised me with his look. I expected him to withdraw in rejection. What he did was say, "I respect that, and Naomi, I love you. I want you to be my wife." Julius did not push or badger. He immediately accepted what I said and held on to me with such reassurance. I was like, "What the hell just happened?" I did not say it aloud; instead I lowered my head in shame. As I allowed my head to drop, Julius reached over and grabbed my neck with affection and kissed me softly on my lips. I pursued his restoration and kissed him back gently. We didn't speak of marriage anymore that visit, and I was comforted in that I had dodged the question.

I returned home feeling both energized and drained. Julius' presence always fired me up. It was like stirring a pot of well-simmered soup, with each lift the aroma is more robust, and the steam warms your insides without even being consumed. I was energized in our love. Knowing someone loves you makes you stronger, richer and bolder. Julius loved me and I him. I was strong and even bold until someone kneeled in front of me on bended knee with "Will you marry me?" Julius was not on his knees physically, but his heart put him there all the same. I heard it dance and skip across my brain, and my boldness began to diminish. It retreated along with my thoughts of *Not now*. I forced marriage to the back and far side of possibility. I in place reflected and thought solely of the here and now of being in love. I love you. I love you. I love you. Love is what it does. I loved Julius with a "Not now."

I didn't focus on my faux pas of that summer visit. After all, I was in love. And what feels even better was a tall, handsome black man loved me too. Life was good in steady exchange with Julius' I love you.

I couldn't get enough of it, and neither could he. The initial greetings of our letters dawned it; with the following in-betweens with some of the most intense foreplay we could have with the mailman being of service. And it ended with the knowledge and certainty that love had not left, and it was accompanied by "missing you." The velocity of our writing had nothing on the volume. Julius and I poured out parts of lives past, present and future in plenty. There was a harvest of sharing; I loved him all the more. His consistent company warmed that cold winter.

I was still crazy in love, so I braved the unpredictable Western New York weather and traveled to see him after the Thanksgiving holiday. After all the heavy petting of the summer, I was anxiously awaiting just a slight hug. We had been in drought of each other's touch for almost three months. I was a kid on Christmas morning when I saw Julius walk through the door of that visiting room. He approached me blushing so that only I could see how much he desired me. We had seats almost near the rear of the visiting room. We were just another couple scattered in the multitude. Julius hugged me tight in response to how securely I held him. We sat, and he smiled. I loved to see his smile because he rationed it like limited nourishing resources after a famine. Julius' smile is so much younger than his years, and it has all the innocence and sincerity of a kindergartner. His smile is both mischievous and carefree. It is like the ease of a rainbow in the sky, beautiful and glowing while humbly blending and floating into the thickness of the air. Julius is fine and he's mine, so I smile back.

We talked and kissed. He grabbed my warmth with his cold hands, and I said as I always had, "Your hands are cold." It didn't cause Julius to withdraw; he just sought more of my warmth.

"I've been missing you," he said. "You're such a cutie and you know it."

"Cute is for monkeys," was the remark I gave him the first time he referred to me as that. I was really crazy now, because I was clinging and swinging to all affections he gave me. He would extend his hand, and without another cue or word, I would extend mine in reception. Julius would say "I" and I would continue "love you," in unison and agreement. I was for real in love. If Julius asked of me, it almost shall be done. If he wanted, I intended to meet the need.

I hadn't seen him in months while at the same time we had many erotic experiences. We had created a new level to phone sex. My orgasm had gone from the stimulation of an intense kiss to call and response of lead musical extraordinaire with gifted prodigy. He would say, "In one inch, and bring it almost out." The master musician was playing every note as a true virtuoso, and my strings' melody represented his consummate skills. Julius knew the whole ten-minute repertoire instinctively and played it deliberately with many variations that always left me singing my concerto orchestrated by him and with him. I called Julius' name followed by "I love you." And finally we were in the visiting room after months of physically being apart, and I was foolishly in love.

We began sharing meals almost after the first few visits more than a year ago. He was eating and drinking after me, and that was gross in his mind, but he did it willingly. He would feed me bites of food and eat right after me, using the same fork. It was nothing for him to quench my thirst with the first sip and then make the cup or bottle communal to our table. We were extensions of each other, and sharing was natural.

On this cold day in the visiting room, we had eaten and talked about all the things that required our immediate attention. We even had a few jokes and much laughter at first. Somewhere past midway through the visit, all jokes were set aside and the hand holding led us into another space. We were quiet in the onset of that moment. Julius swears that by nature he is quiet and not much for conversation. But in the midst of our visits, he seemed contrary to that description. He talked almost nonstop, and sometimes I would tell him just that. Over time, he shared with me that it was his way to control the mood of the visit. My silence often led to exposing the hurt and anxiety of our separation. I never intended to descend to that melancholy place. I think it was allowed to be revealed because of fatigue and the sheer necessity to be genuine with each other. On this day, I was not descending to the emotional well of apartness or loss. I was dispatching to a familiar place that was reserved for quiet and secluded places. I was in a room alone with Julius that just happened to be occupied with more than 120 other people. We were engaged in each other's presence. He embraced my hands, and I was covered in him just by the physical connection. Julius did not kiss me at that moment. He was clearing his throat to begin his routine lengthy talk about something—any something. I leaned into him, and I kissed him. My temperature felt like it shot straight to 101, and there was no shade. There was nothing to cover, hide or secure us. He did not refuse me, restrain me or even restrict me from having access to him. We were connecting, which was not neighboring or bordering. It was much like I stepped into his secluded space and he into mine. They were one, and we were in trouble. How do you cool down combustion? We breathed air into the fire, and the flames roared. My pulse began to beat out of my body. I was hot in a cold visiting room. This hot flash was Julius induced, and I wanted to shed any semblance of incalescence. I was sweltering, and he was losing his stronghold to fight me off. I could feel Julius' lips trying to tell me to stop or to close to keep my tongue from opening secret places far beyond his mouth. The next word he said should have been *stop*. Instead what I heard was, "Unbutton your blouse." I didn't hear my conscience say "no," "hold on," "slow down," "wait a minute" or any words to derail our current course. I exhaled and kissed him. In my kiss, I repositioned myself to scoot back in the chair while adjusting my sweater closer to me. I continued the kiss all in one harmonious motion. I unbuttoned two buttons in the middle of my blouse. They created access without exposure. Julius, almost like a good magician, caressed my breast through the satin overlay of my bra. My nipples become engorged. Every part of me wanted to be full from his touch. He moaned as he felt the fullness of my breast, and I was hot and possibly on my way to hell or at least out of that visiting room through non-voluntary methods. It felt so good. I had not been touched in such a long time. He both stroked gently and applied pressure from his thumb and forefinger to my hardness. I was trying to stay still, but I did not release from his embrace. His breathing increased, and he had exposed my right breast to view. His mouth was wet and his lips were hot. As I leaned into his open legs, I felt his erection against my knee. Oh Lord … I was so in trouble.

"Girl, have you lost your mind?" "You are acting just plain trifling up in a prison visiting room." "Naomi, I taught you better." My mother's voice must have been so loud that Julius heard it too. He separated us so he could breathe. My conscience was in the tone of Melody, my mother. She went on to say, "I know my private school money taught you more than that." Julius looked of pain and pleasure all at once. He shook his head to the rhythm of "Mmm, mmm, mmm" as he licked his lips very slowly. At this point both breasts were visible to him, and his eyes had widened to his delight. He did not speak, and neither did I. I was ashamed and proud all at the same time. I was ashamed because I thought how unladylike of me. I was ashamed because I was putting myself in a compromising position. I was ashamed because I was in a prison visiting room with my blouse open and all the fullness of my breasts hanging like ripen fruit ready to be plucked. I was unashamed because the man I love delighted in me. I was taking pleasure in his satisfaction. I was proud of my love for him, no matter how irrational my actions may have seemed. I loved Julius and everything in me needed him to know that. I did not open my blouse solely to his command. I unbuttoned it to create an entrance for him to love me. We sat for a short time in that gaze, and as he accessed the entryway, at the same time he closed my blouse and hugged me. He held my back as he whispered, "Let me fix your clothes." I felt the completeness of his erection still in place as he repositioned my breasts back into their harness. I did not wrap my hands over his in understanding. Instead I allowed him to complete our anomalous lovemaking. He made love to me that day for the first time. When our passions exceeded their ability or liberties, Julius simply loved me back with respect. After he buttoned the last button, he pulled my sweater to, as if he was sealing away pleasure for a later date.

The hours had flown by on this visit. Our kiss good-bye seemed more somber but more whole than it had ever been. I knew that the likelihood of me seeing him again before the welcome of the New Year was almost none. We were one of the last couples to leave the visiting room that day. He wrapped his arms around me and held me close as we waited for the visiting slip and inmate IDs to be returned to the rightful holders.

I drove another silent drive home. I felt the tears form in my eyes as I tried to make sense of the day's activities. I asked myself if I would have really been willing to risk our visits and embarrass or astonish all those people in the visiting room that day if we had been observed and caught by the officers. I loved him, but did that give me the right to break institution's rules or degrade myself in front of others. I did not accept the degradation theory because my intent was not to dishonor myself or act out of accordance with forms of dignity. I simply wanted the man I love to have expressions of that. I talked to him on the way home.

"Julius, do you know how much I love you?" He could not answer since he was not there. "Julius, do you know how much it hurts to put my car in park in the lot of this prison? Babe, when I get out of the car, I try to untangle the nerves in my stomach and unbind the lump in my throat." I continued my talk to him. "I hate this prison. I hate you being in a prison. I hate the separation. I hate the time. Julius, do you know how much I love you?"

I had talked my tired self all the way home. I had gone through four toll booths—the two to gain access to that portion of the highway and the two to exit. When I got home, I removed my clothes down to my bareness. I stood naked in front of the bedroom mirror. I tried to see what Julius saw. I stood there and tried to visualize how he felt. I could not make my face find favor the way he did. He enjoyed and sought out my nakedness. I crossed my arms over my breasts and held myself as I rolled into bed. The coolness of my heavy tears sprinkled down the warmth of my face. I placed my hands between my legs and turned over to my side. I held myself that night in hopes of Julius being there and did not release until I was into the depth of sleep.

The winter seemed extremely long that year. Julius and I wrote, but we spoke very little of that day in the visiting room. Our phone conversations were soon cut off by a block from MCI. Our sexcapades had landed us a phone bill in excess of nine hundred dollars. I decided that the sacrifice to pay that bill was greater than the current need, so we were back to correspondence by mail only. Julius did not complain about the phone. I know he missed it. He missed hearing me calling his name and the gentle moans that were reserved for him. He probably even missed his delegation of sexual entry over the phone. But most of all we missed each other's voices. We wrote letters that still were heavy with "I love you" in the beginning, everyday current affairs in the middle and finished with the real truth of "I love you, and I miss you."

As the New Year was fast approaching, Julius began to look forward to his first parole appearance. And in my naïveté, I was too. I looked forward to parole because I expected that if he did the time, he was coming home. By then we had professed "I love you" probably more than a thousand times separately. Before the New Year came, Julius asked me to marry him. I did not hesitate to say yes, although we had spent time not talking about getting married directly, but more about why I would wait. Because I was not in New York, his upcoming parole would force us to talk more heavily about living in different states.

We had discussed the possibilities of paroling to Ohio, and they were limited to relocation by every parole guideline we had read. Our plans of life together were real, and we were watering and nourishing them with every opportunity we had. Shortly after Christmas, he asked me to marry him again, and he followed it up with the requirements to get married in a New York prison. The fee was twenty-five dollars to be paid to the town clerk. I would have to have a marriage interview with a counselor, all of which was possible only if the superintendent approved our letter of request. On January 21, I wrote that letter and mailed in my request to marry Julius after the license, which expired in sixty days, was issued. It was happening very fast because by mid-February I had already had the marriage interview, and my big deal breaker was not having a reverend to marry us. The process itself is not rigorous, but it does not go smoothly or without delay.

The weather held nicely for me to make the drive to Western New York before the conclusion of winter. I arrived at the facility with a twenty-five-dollar money order and my birth certificate. I was so incredibly nervous. It was far beyond jitters. Julius seemed to arrive in the visiting room in probably one fourth of his normal time. It seemed like I sat down, and he walked in the door within fifteen minutes of my arrival. In reality it was almost fifty minutes later. My heart was racing, and his excitement seemed to be as accelerated as my anxiety. He kissed me, and he was on cloud nine. We were waiting for the town clerk to arrive so that we could be ushered into a broom closet–sized room to complete the papers for the marriage license. The town clerk was excited as most people who are associated with the launch of a wedding.

She greeted us both and introduced herself as Mrs. Montero. She began our meeting by requesting our full names, dates of birth and parent information, all of which was routine. She made small talk while transposing our information onto the form. Julius was excited, and I could feel his legs moving up and down in an unconscious quick rhythmic motion. I was sitting at the edge of my seat, leaning forward, watching her write every letter in its proper position. Julius held my hand as young lovers do, with confidence that this process would go quickly and as prepared and planned. Everything was full speed ahead until Mrs. Montero asked, "Dear, what will your last name be after the marriage? Will you keep it the same, take his surname or hyphenate?" I think I stopped breathing, and I am not sure for how long because when I looked directly at her, she was looking at me, and the pen was at a standstill. I know the pen stopped in alliance with Julius' leg motions. My articulation was out the little door of that room, and I think I was rambling or mumbling because she looked as if she was trying to read my lips. The words finally tumbled out of my mouth, and I replied, "Um, hyphenate." Julius wore a surprised expression, which was only recognizable by me. He released his hold on my hand and rubbed my arm, just as Mrs. Montero said, "That will be twenty-five dollars." I put the envelope that rested on my lap on top of the desk, removed the money order and slid it to her. Julius relaxed in his chair, almost motionless. Mrs. Montero explained that we were to contact the facility to either schedule with the justice of the peace (JP) or get a referral of the ministers who already had access to the facility. She congratulated us as we exited that tiny windowless office.

Julius walked the short distance back to our visiting room table behind me with his right hand gently on my shoulder. He pulled my chair out to allow me to sit. He sat and exhaled a long breath while leaning forward on the table. He put both hands together in front of him and asked, "What was that?"

I replied as if I was mystified, "What was what?"

He responded, "Back there you were shook when that lady asked about your name. We talked before this, and I explained everything to you. I told you to ask me any question and I would tell you anything you wanted or needed to know."

I sat in silence, leaning forward with my chair slightly apart from the table. Julius continued, "I wanted you to be prepared and not have any questions or doubts on what you are getting into. I've never lied to you because I want this marriage to work." At this point he was annoyed, but restrained from all-out anger.

I was self-absorbed in "I just signed to get married," but I vaguely understood his disappointment.

I heard him say last before his sigh, "What made you decide to hyphenate your name?"

I couldn't manage a response because I hadn't given it enough thought to have a well-examined answer. *It felt right,* was my initial thought because I had clung to Naomi Hill for thirty-something years. That's all I had known, and it somehow had more power and presence than the new name alone. I did not plan to leave that question uninvestigated, unexplained nor misunderstood, but at that present date it would not be the education and research process to give an accurate answer. I was aware that I was going to marry inside a prison.

The remainder of that visit was awkward and ironic for a couple who was planning to spend their lives together. I don't remember much after that visit, other than my instructions to Julius: "You need to find all the names of the reverends who can marry us." He promised to ask around the facility and write me in the upcoming week. Although he was bewildered with my behavior, disappointed with my answer and still trying to understand my reasoning, he kissed me good-bye with a promise of a lifetime together.

As I walked out of the facility, I turned to look at him in his seat. His body language was unfamiliar to me. Julius looked like he had the weight of the world on his shoulders. I could not help him because I had the weight of the world on my heart.

The remainder of February and even into late March was full of a late winter hangover. Julius was not making much headway with the reverend, and I began calling on my own. I did not have a clue what to look for or where to seek answers. The facility finally provided two names. The first one was no longer in the area. We were now down to one option, Reverend Wilkes.

I called Reverend Wilkes twice with no reply. After the third call, there would be no more, as that was my rule. The final time was my lucky evening because I caught him at home. He was rude and cold within our first few sentences. I began the conversation with my introduction and anticipated that this man of the cloth would offer some divine wisdom, guidance and criteria for marriage. I received none of that. What I got instead was, "I need seventy-five dollars in advance sent at least two weeks prior to the wedding. On the day of the wedding, you will need to have seventy-five dollars, payable by money order." I did not allow him to finish because I was appalled at his initial response. We exchanged several more formalities and concluded the conversation. I hung up the phone feeling disillusioned and betrayed. I told Julius of my experience, and he offered the justice of the peace or for me to call around to locate another minister. I felt the need to replay my strong desire to have a reverend marry us, as I truly wanted God's blessing on our marriage. I was adamant about not having a civil representative marry us as they are the same civil people who assist in divorce. I desperately needed to feel God's power in this decision.

After five full weeks had passed, we needed to make a decision because everyone's calendar had to be taken into consideration. The JP had a sixty-five-dollar fee, and he had specific days for availability. I ran from his services and what I thought it stood for. Julius appeared to be patient, but in his letters I could feel his rising animosity. All he wanted was for me to be his wife, and whatever I needed to make it so, he wanted to be able to provide that. I boldly held on to my single request for a minister. I did not fight for it, work diligently for it or renege on it. It was almost April, and the license would expire before the end of the month.

Through this whole search for a reverend, Julius' hands were tied. He had no access to help in locating my one petition, as his sole resource was other inmates who were married by the JP or the imam. I rejected both. It was solely up to me to advance the wedding or more importantly our marriage, and my feet felt like they were ice cold with the feeling of being stuck in quicksand. I was going to marry an inmate, and I had not come to terms with that.

Julius suspected my fears and questioned, "Are you ashamed of me?"

It was such an explicit question, and I replied, "I am not ashamed of you, but I'm not proud of where you are."

For the first time in our relationship, I was being dishonest by playing a word game. I felt our marriage would be inadequate. In my mind we were incapable of being a whole couple; we were sliced and diced because he temporarily belonged to the state of New York. All thoughts of my husband being held should have been connected to me, not the Department of Corrections.

I was feeling the heaviness of emotional quicksand, neither willing to move forward and cherishing all the steps that were behind. I was stuck. The only thing I knew with certainty was I was not letting Julius go. We and our relationship were under unsupported stress. There wasn't a way, a place or people who would become pores to allow the stress of what was going on inside of us to be released. We were saturated, and I did not know how to tell him that I needed abatement. All the love we had was on the line. I was hurting, and he was not the source of my pain but his situation was administering without mercy. How do you say to the man you love, "I am scared?" I have no answer for that because I never told him, although his keen insight apprised him of such.

Julius as strong and forthright as he had always been did not inquire anymore. Over the few years that we had been fostering our relationship, I had witnessed and learned of his frustration, disappointment and abandonment from other family members and friends. He had taught himself how to manage his loss. Julius would simply calculate the loss and move on without looking back. As the days crept along to the end of April, Julius experienced one of his greatest afflictions. At my hands, he would feel the distress of emotional abandonment. I held on tightly to save me from the sinking sands, and he anchored himself on the surrounding shore, not willing to move one inch. Julius did not let go, but he was no longer going to struggle to keep me. If I wanted out of the sand, I would have to trust him enough to make the next move.

I wounded him so deeply that he withdrew and took key things back in preparation to move on. Julius wrote me one of the most profound statements that let me know this was true. His words were: "I am returning to Islam. It will not leave me." He came straight at me, not with maliciousness, but full force with questioning who I was. Julius' statement challenged my belief and more so the excuse for our wedding not occurring. The minister or lack thereof was not the root cause; it was merely the symptom of my fear. His plan to return to Islam was an exit strategy and a method to abbreviate his emotional casualty, had we not been able to salvage and sustain this relationship. He also requested that I return some of his most cherished photographs that had been entrusted to me until his homecoming. I was going to have to fight for this relationship, his trust and our friendship. The only thing on which I could hang my hat of hope was he truly loved me, but I was painfully aware that sometimes immature love is not enough.

At this time, we were both battling for a future, and he was mounting his defense for his release. August would be his first shot at being paroled. The initial appearance was more of a blessing than the obvious curse of his sentence not being commuted. Because Julius engaged and committed himself absolutely to whatever goal was forefront and center, he placed most of his energy and efforts into his parole package.

During the parole process, he couldn't afford negative energy from my moment of rejection, so he set me aside emotionally for his own well-being. This was different for Julius on many levels. He had never been one for forgiveness and restoration. He had been a person to offer you that single shot. He is an "if you mess up, then you're gone" kind of guy. For one of the few times in his life, he was not prepared to turn his back on someone and walk away. I was simply set aside, and it allowed me to work at regaining his trust.

He still loved me and told me so, but I was no longer his only focus. Julius had laid all his cards on my table, and it was up to me to even the odds. I did reassure him that I wasn't going anywhere, but past experience had labeled my statement as empty words. I needed to prove to him that I was committed to him and a future. We worked on his parole package, and I was more than the woman of his pursuit. I was an investor and on my way to partner in his life. We assembled an impressive package to be presented to the group of three who were charged to decide if he was ready to be released back into society.

During that preparation, we had to work as a team, and on occasion his mistrust, doubt and anger with me would show up. He did not want me to leave, but he wasn't sure if I would stay. He would often get short or angry with me if he hadn't received something he requested in his undisclosed time-frames. Julius restrained as much as he could in part because he understood me and my needs, but mostly because he didn't have the energy for it. I supported and loved him through this process.

The beginning of August brought anxiety, tension, hope and more questions. We clung to each other and became better friends. On a stormy Friday evening in mid-August, I received a phone call from his sister, Dana. It was almost 9:30 that evening, and I was driving from Quincy's performance in the final production of his summer camp. I was alone, and that was good. Dana said, "Julius wanted me to call you and tell you he was denied. He wants me to make sure you are alright. He sounds fine. Are you okay?"

"Um, I need to go. Thanks. Bye."

I did not allow her one more courtesy or word. I dropped the phone to my feet and looked for a place to pull over off the highway. It had stormed very heavily earlier that evening with almost four inches of rain accompanied by fierce thunder and lightning. Not many cars were on the road. I was less than five miles from home, yet my emotional breakdown would not allow me another minute to drive. I stopped my car on the side of the road and began to wail. I cried and screamed and the word, *Why?* formed on my lips, but was held captive in my month against sniffles and the pant to catch my breath. I ached inside and out. I cried so hard and fought to restrain myself. The war had caused an immediate casualty, and my head felt like it would explode. I don't know how long I sat on the side of the road. I know I cried until I felt like I had depleted all the water in my body, and I was exhausted. I drove the few miles to my home and walked inside what was to be our home and dropped all that was hanging on me to the floor. Jewel was excited at my arrival, and I pushed the door open to his freedom. He ran around my legs, bumping and jumping with excitement. I did not reward him. He ran outdoors, and I stood. Upon his return, I closed the door, turned off the lights and climbed the stairs, which felt monstrous. I plopped into the bed fully clothed, including my shoes. I was still for a moment and then the replenished tears began to fall. I forced myself into the darkness of sleep because that was all I could do. Before I drifted to sleep, I cried out once more, "God, why?" I prayed. "Why?"

The morning after, the day after, the week after were hard, yet forgettable. I was walking through the days, and I was angry. Julius' concern for me was probably greater than his own, and he focused on my pain. I could not express to anyone how much hurt I felt and the depth of my loss. I did not allow the loss to belong to us—selfishly it was mine alone. Julius held on to me, and I received his consoling the following week on a visit. I drove to New York auto-matically. I did not think or plan. All I knew was I needed to be at the burial site of my hope, our recent future and my naïveté. He walked to me and held me with such protection. I was not a giver that day. I took all that Julius had, and it drained him. He knew that I was broken and wounded, so he disguised his disappointment and mended his friend. I fought tears the entire visit, and he countered and soothed me with plans of appeal. I couldn't really listen, but I heard him. I knew that my loss was no greater or less than; Julius elevated mine and covered his. That day I had a profound awareness that we were in this together.

Julius solicited legal aid and drafted his appeal brief. He told the law firm that I was his wife so that I could gain access to his case's proceedings, unre-served for non-family members. I followed up and stayed in constant contact with them to the point that I annoyed the primary counsel. Nonetheless, they completed and mailed the brief off for the 120-day wait for a reply. Julius and I did not focus on the appeal; instead we worked on healing us.

Julius saw something in the parole and appeal preparation that made him step back from the marriage and cherish our friendship. Almost from the onset of that initial three-way phone conversation he was focused on us getting mar-ried and me becoming his wife. I think we both communicated things from our past that disclosed and revealed who and where we were in fostering a love relationship. We were friends by default instead of friends by design. After experiencing such a shattering loss, we had to re-create the dreams and rede-sign the plans for our lives separately and hopefully together. Somewhere in the midst of the denial or delay were two people who knew how to survive. Julius came to a point where he no longer wanted to discuss marriage, and I recognized its familiarity from the first time he asked me to marry him. He had received patience as a virtue when dealing with me. This allowed him to hold his place while waiting for me to see and receive the vision. I was in many ways a slow learner, but once I got it, I became a great teacher.

Much to no one's surprise, the appeal decision came back on the 119th day. It upheld the parole boards' decision, and we were well into the next year and several months of the twenty-four-month reappearance date. Julius was rest-less, so he requested to transfer. This would be yet another facility for me to learn, but it was also an opportunity for him to learn other trades through dif-ferent programs. We had no control over in what part of New York he would end up. The hope was for him to get closer to me and back to the first facility where our relationship began. That was not the case. He got closer to the city—he was now more than six hundred miles away.

If absence makes the heart grow fonder, then distance makes the connection deeper. I wanted and needed to see him desperately, but random or unplanned visits were no longer an option. His relocation to the Hudson Valley of New York rejuvenated him in the beauty of his new surroundings. He was in one of the most unified and educated facilities in the state. Experience breeds knowledge, and he found many other inmates who had way too much experience with denials in the parole process. Another gem that was destined to meet his acquaintance was a rare, seasoned counselor, Mrs. Carry. For the three years that I had been his constant companion, he had never spoken of any counselor who actually wanted to hear his ideas in his rehabilitation process. He met this one and became more focused and driven on becoming better, no matter where he was. I loved to hear it in his letters and his voice. We had phone privileges back through a creative and generous person. I was now able to talk to Julius twice a month at Alex, who was unaware of such, and Simone's house. I was giddy. He was encouraged, and our love sparked; now flames of our passion that before glowed a faint blue ember were now outlined in red with gentles hues of orange and a dazzling yellow core. I missed Julius, and I began to plan my visit for mid-August. As the weeks slowly waltzed by, my anticipation of seeing his countenance grew stronger. I had not felt his coolness in my warmth for almost six months. That was the longest we had ever gone without each other's physical touch.

I intended to make the ten-hour drive alone, but my cousin and best friend would not allow it. My cousin Myeisha, the one who has always been there for me, in her sisterly protectiveness offered to go with me. She agreed to keep me company and help drive. We laughed, talked and sang along with the CDs that we had brought. The ride went smooth, and we reached our destination at two o'clock in the morning. I could not sleep in eager anticipation of seeing my love. She could not sleep because it was one of the worst hotels in which I had ever stayed. I hated her discomfort, but it was a small price to pay to be with the man I loved.

I awoke at 5:45 that morning, showered and pampered myself for this long-awaited visit. While I had become accustomed and familiar with the rules to enter a New York prison, I still had anxiety and nervousness before each visit. The beautiful and charming ride in the hills had not changed that. This facility was different from any of the others that I had visited. It was gated from the time you drove your car onto the premises. An officer checked your vehicle and

ID before he provided you a number and entry to the grounds. I drove to the door and entered yet another prison. The people were nicer than most, and they had more of that hard New York City accent of dragging out the last syllable and altering its vowel sound. This visiting room sat high off the ground with lots of windows and lights bouncing and contrasting its dark wood. The room was larger than many and very square. It seemed more open than any other previously visited place because of the high open ceiling. I was able to select my seating in this almost empty room. I sat close to the sunlight that was shining through all the tiny windowpanes. When Julius walked in, my heart began to dance in the sunshine and take on its glow. He had to walk from his entranceway all the way to the opposite end of the room to give the officer his ID. I watched him glide in both gratitude and appreciation. Julius was beautiful, he was splendid, and I was madly in love. By the time he reached our table, I was standing and beaming from ear to ear. I held him so tight and breathed in his scent. He smiled and I said, "I love you" before I kissed him. He had to know that—he needed to know that. We visited very much like many times before. We dined at the vending machines and enjoyed our communal feast. We talked, and he allowed me to rest in his arms as he massaged my head. I was comforted in him, and we were healing.

I was able to visit him the following day before my departure for the ten-hour ride back. He held my hands in his coolness and caressed my arms. He pulled all of me into him as he hugged me. It was as if he could not get all he wanted but more than he hoped for. We had many moments of delicate and deliberate silence. We found each other in every moment of that visit. I knew his love, and it was stronger and bolder than ever before. I found my boldness in him, and my love was stronger too. The good-bye had more promise than ever before. Although, I was farther away in distance from where he laid his head and where I laid mine, we were never more a part of each other. I hugged and held him, never wanting to let go and telling him that as I prepared to leave. We had no idea when we would see each other again because it was late fall and he was too great a distance for random travel. I left a part of me there that day, but it was not missed, just on loan.

The drive back was sadder for me, and Myeisha noticed it. She said abruptly, "Are you in love?"

"Duh," would have been my response but I ached too much and was depleted.

"Yes." That's all I said for a while, and my silence made her uncomfortable. She glanced at me as she drove, and I slouched in the reclined passenger seat.

She kept looking over like she was checking if I was ill, so I told her of the plans to marry him. I continued to explain that we would have been the only ones to know of our marriage and just had a wedding when he was released. She said, "I'm surprised that you're not already married. I kind of thought you were the way you were willing to come all this way just to visit him."

Myeisha and I talked more, but less about Julius. I wanted to keep him close, secure and secluded with me for a little while longer.

By the beginning of September, I could not imagine my life without Julius, and I told him that. He wanted no part of that conversation and had reconciled himself to the fact that if we were to marry it would be upon his release. Julius and I would talk about all the firsts of a newly liberated man, and he would have no list of things to do or restaurants in which he wanted to dine. His sole spoken desire was to make love to me as his wife. He didn't know how it would work or where the person to solemnize our union would be found, but before he intimately touched me through sexual intercourse, we would be married.

I did not put much thought in his release because I was aware of the game. Doing the time was not the issue, the question or the conversation. It was about making him pay with whatever they could take from him, and time was the most priceless possession. I began to entertain marrying him, and I could envision him as my husband the way I was never able to before. He still wanted no part of my foolishness because he was playing for keeps, and it was put up or shut up.

At the beginning of October, I asked him to fast with me for seven days. We had never successfully intertwined our beliefs, and I needed to feel close to him in a spiritual way. I asked him to list three things to put before God during our time of fasting. We were to write each other each day of the fast after we had mailed our three items to each other. I received his list, and he received mine, and they were identical in both content and priority. From his letters, he did not take the fast as seriously as I did, nonetheless he fasted with me. By the fifth day, I had an indescribable desire to marry him and an accompanying peace with the decision. I had never felt anything like it, and I shared that with Julius. He dismissed it for earnestness. By late October, I was seeing no forms in the mail regarding the marriage process. I asked him again, and he said, "I didn't think you were serious. Let me ask, and I'll get back to you." He must have been exorcising his demons of past hurt because by the beginning of November I had no superintendent name and no requirements for marriage. By mid-November, he finally had done what was asked, and the information arrived. On November 18, I wrote my second letter to a superintendent requesting to marry Julius. Mrs. Carry made sure everything went expeditiously. We were approved and scheduled to get married on January 1. The New Year was bringing all the promise and hope of new life. I was going to marry my soul mate. I courted him with little hand-made notes and gifts. I sent him an invitation to our wedding that had our pictures on the front and the wedding vows that we wrote for each other tucked away neatly inside. There were no rules or ultimatum attached. I simply wanted to marry Julius. And I intended to do just that. Our love was now more mature and able to sustain some adversity. We were educated by experience. We were learning how to relieve the pressure or at least share the load. I was prepared to be his wife. He had pulled us through the quicksand as I worked on me and my fears. I knew crazy, foolish and madness. I was now simply in love. I was ready to say, "I pledge," "I promise," "I will" or "I do" to whoever had the power vested in them to make us husband and wife. Love is what love does.

God truly gave me a gift when he brought you into my life.

You are the reason I believe in love again.

I can't image life without you.

Thank you for loving me the way that you do.

—*Geo*

My Definition of a Wife

Susan Goins Castro

"… My beloved is mine, and I am his."

—*Song of Solomon 2:16*

Wife means companion, someone I can put my trust in without having to worry about being betrayed.

Wife means friendship, someone I can laugh with, someone I can share my innermost secrets with.

Someone I can cry in front of without losing my self-dignity or being judged as weak.

Wife means someone I can build a future with, reaching and sharing our life goals together.

Wife means someone who puts her faith and trust in you because she believes in your ability to lead her to where we both need to be in our lives.

Wife means someone with whom you can raise a family. She's someone who will nurture your children the right way because she's a reflection of you and your purpose.

I love my wife …

Our lives were dark before we knew of each other.

The Lord blessed us with each other.

She is my blossoming flower

He is my ever-loving soldier.

We fell in love at first sight

Our love bloomed in the moonlight.

—*Terry and Rayna*

Flowers Bloom in the Moonlight

Rhonda L. Harris

Who ever said
Flowers don't bloom in the moonlight
Never knew me and you

The seeds of love were planted
And took hold of life and blossomed
One day in a prison photo room

Our eyes met
Your gaze held me fast
In our silent introduction
Our souls spoke to each other ...
Is this love at last?

We independently asked ourselves
As we wondered on
The very same questions

What is this thing,
This thing that they call love?
Was this love at first sight?

In my quiet reflection I wondered
How does one really know
When it is truly love?

How does one know
That they have met
The one who is "the One"?

Was this merely our need to be needed?
Our need to be loved?
Should we doubt something so special, so magical?
Was it sent from above?

The day we met you held my hand
In a very simple exchange
And then whispered my name
Who would know that this would be
The beginning of our forever romance?

Our worlds were melancholy
Your world, a prison cell
Full of pain, sorrow, disappointment—
Mainly in yourself

My cell out here was a solemn one
Plagued by trials, experiences
That left me trusting no one

We were both afraid
Of exposing our jaded pasts
Not full well knowing if the receiver
Would be willing to accept us and our fate
Would this be the one to last?

Yet my dreams never died
Your dreams kept alive
We always knew that the God above
Would one day, someday
Send us someone to love

Now just look at the awesomeness
And power of love
Of God's love
That has manifested in our lives

Remember when,
You touched my hand
I fell in love
You loved me then

I love to talk about my love for you
To tell the world all about
The awesomeness of you

In this my homage to you
It kind of makes me smile
Not that the loves
From your past
Love did not last
But it is in their choosing
To miss out on the wonder of you
They chose to hide from you
By not being there
Not there for you
Never supporting you
I was rewarded with the gift
Of being loved by you

Please don't misconstrue my feelings
I do not intend to boast
I actually owe them many thanks
And send them blessings too
For had they not turned their backs
I may have never met you

I was the one who didn't let
Those bars surrounding you
Obstruct my view of you
The windows to your soul
Told me all I needed to know

I saw a good man
Whose mistakes cost him his life
I saw a man who learned from them
And lived solely to be a better man
I saw myself as his wife
My first and only true love

From that first phone call I was hooked
I could instantly feel
Your soul, spirit and energy
The entire essence of who you were
And I knew you were meant for me
That we were simply meant to be

I've often sat and wondered
Why is this feeling of love so intense for you
Reflection has lead me to recognize
That the answer lies in oh so many things
It is especially your tender ability
To love me wonderfully
Especially when I don't make it that easy
In spite of how I can be
When I am just being me

You remain the principal member
Of my dream team
The one who knows me like no other
You adore me
My faults

My secrets
Joys and pains
Likes and dislikes
Issues too
Yet you continue to love me
Completely
Unconditionally

The motivation, determination
And drive deep within me
Are kept alive through your continued belief in me
You make me believe that I can do anything
Can conquer the world
Can have anything
You're my number one
Cheerleader
Motivator
Mentor
Protector
Best friend
And lover

Our honeymoon was filled
With immense love, pleasure and
Tenderness
In the way you touched me
So passionately, so tenderly
The tremendous delight of true love
The epitome of commitment
The mutual giving of sharing
One to another in every possible way

This love is returned from me to you
Through my undying belief in you
My encouraging and uplifting you

In every aspect of all you do
This is my devout service to you

I fall in love over and over again
As I progress
From one paragraph to the next

My eyes well up with tears
On this an emotional day
In my talking to the Father
I fell on my knees to pray
Why Father,
Did you send
This amazing man to me
But keep him far from me?
As I cried
My sorrow was interrupted
By the ringing of the phone
It was you—my one true love
I asked you the same question
That I posed to Our Father above

In your reply you said
"Sweetheart, you are my destiny
And I am yours for eternity
He knew exactly what I needed
And He gave me you
And He placed treasures in me
Exclusively for you
In the fulfilling of our purpose
He allowed our paths cross
In order to receive this miracle
We would endure great pain
To whom much is given

Much is required
Have we not fulfilled one another's desire?"

Today as I recall your loving reply
I still often ask why
Why does this love have to hurt so bad?
Why does this pain of separation
From the one I love
Cause me such agony
And make me so sad?

Killing me slowly is how a friend
Today
Described the life of an inmate's wife
Today, a husband was denied parole
The more I thought about it
The more my own tears fell
Feeling love, feeling pain
And grave disappointment
Helplessness and hopelessness
Anger, frustration and sorrow
The shattered dreams for today
The shattered dreams of tomorrow
My tears fell for us all
For her, her husband and family
For those who have been denied
For those who will be denied
Killing me slowly
Today that very well describes
The life of an inmate's wife

I know that I often
Throw such things at you
Never really probing for an answer
Just seeking some understanding

Trying to release the frustration
With hopes of finding a brighter view
Yet today the view is cloudy and gray
Because at this very moment
I am experiencing
The joy of being in love
And the pain of being apart
I try to find comfort in knowing
That there must be some meaning
In all that we go through
So I cling to believing
That we are enduring
All of this madness
Toward a purpose that must be fulfilling

The days spent apart are
Extremely hard and painful
The days spent together
Always joyous and meaningful
And it is the culmination of all those days
That gives me the fortitude
To keep fighting
Fighting to go on

Don't you know that I sit back
And count down the days
Until you are home with me?

Don't you know that I often
Cry myself to sleep
Because I am longing for you
To hold me as "we" fall asleep?

To have found love
Yet be separated from it

Some sick joke this has to be!
I get so sick of wishing
This life to be over

I still do not know
What is to be learned in finding love
But not allowed to live it completely

Without the help of friends
I know I couldn't go on
Strength has been here to hold me up
When I can't do it for myself
He is there when I must battle
My way through the downs
And every phase of depression
That tries to conquer
Tear me down

You and strength keep me together
And never let me fall
I could not live this life without you all

My goal is not to feel badly
I just want to be closer to you
There are days
When I think I can't continue
Then all of a sudden miraculously
My thoughts of you
Help me realize
That it is all about you
Because you make it happen for me
And even as crazy as this life can be
I do find comfort in loving you
Through this crazy and unpredictable journey

I feel you in my spirit every day
I feel your loving embrace
Your heartfelt kisses
Our closeness
My love for you
Your love for me
The power of His blessing

Okay
I have to dry my eyes
And smile because I see
Visions of you
Before me, next to me, with me
And the joy that you bring me

Time has revealed so many things
Over these many years
Others always want to know
What is it about that man?
My love for you is one thing though
That really can't be explained
It is that kind of thing that is just all-knowing
We are so in tune with each other
We had that instant comfort and familiarity
Our like kind spirits attracted to the other
Our spirituality being there
I love the love we share
The love we make each day
Through our written and spoken words
Our souls connecting in every way

The things I love most about you
Are all enclosed inside of you
Everything that you have done

Those things that you've been through
Everything that you will do

At the top of my list
Is your ability to be
So loving, caring
And most important, God-fearing
Now that is so sexy to me
To see my man on his knees
Praying to the Father above
For my safety and protection
And thanking Him for the gift of our love

You know what else turns me on?
When I just watch how you
Care for me and for our girls
You are often vulnerable, even
And always undeniably warm
It is your gentleness that I adore
The depths of our love makes me feel
Like I'm at Heaven's door

Love's exquisite freedom
We are captive and also free
Love's exquisite freedom
Between you and me
It is simply being free to be
Free from hurt and pain
Free from dishonesty
Free from betrayal
Free from loneliness
And most importantly
It just means
You being free to be

Me being free to be me
Just being free to be

Tears still well up in my eyes
When I reminisce and even fantasize
Of our loving times
The times of joy when we began
The time of our first rendezvous
Our passionate intimate union
My yielding to you in an instant
So enticing, so inviting
I spend so many of my waking days
Thinking of you
Looking at you
Dreaming about you
Simply loving you
My dreams are always engrossed
With visions and thoughts of you

Most recently I had a dream
Of our making love
It was so real
So real I could feel and see
Visions of you
Thoroughly encapsulating me
The dream was one of us
Becoming one

My fires always burn
For you of course
Some nights are so much worse
Craving for your body those nights
Keeps sleep at bay at night
The longing to be closer to you
Feeling your heart

Beating against mine
Envisioning
Your broad shoulders
That I hold on tightly to
When we combine in harmony
Your ass that I grab forcefully
When I am guiding you deeper
Into my pleasure zone
Your strong legs that support me
When loving maneuvers
Take us beyond our natural course
Your perfect gorgeous dick
That gives me great pleasure
Intensely, immensely, repeatedly
You make love to me so tenderly
That it brings tears to my eyes
You kiss me passionately
And enter me so gently
Every inch of you taking over me
It is days like these
Especially
That I miss you and
Our sexual energy
Excite the very essence
Of passion within each other
Intense love, passion and energy
Culminates in our lovemaking
Resulting in adventures of ecstasy
Beauty and mesmerizing love
It is days like these
That I wish you were here
Then we could be
In each other's arms

Making love
Physically
Expressing
Love

I never knew being in love
Would feel this good
How can I not be in love?
With my knight
Who when he gazes at me
Calls me his "marvelous wonder"
His queen
His heroine
His bright light
His guiding light
His restoration of hope

When he looks into my eyes
And reveals that paradise
Is anywhere that I am
How can I not be in love?

My heart fluttered
When I heard you say
That you would marry me
Every day

I love the inner workings of your mind
I love your heart of gold
I love the gift you give to others
How you comfort and console your brothers
Even during your own time of need

Every year of loving you
Has been heightened
By our operating

In the veins of reflection
Rekindling and rejoicing in
Our spiritual connection
Our irreversible, unbreakable bond
Coupled together by the Almighty
His will binding us together
Forever
Knowing that we were created
One for the other

How blessed and loved we are
Many go through life never knowing
A love that is overwhelming
The ultimate depths of love
The one thing that I know
If I don't know anything else
I know that I am blessed
I know who loves me
Cares for me
Cherishes me
Adores me
Honors me
Nurtures me
Protects me
Covers me
Wants me
Needs me
Deserves me

I thank God every day
For the will and capability
For being in love

This is such a blessing to behold
We stand forever grateful, thankful

For his guidance
Direction
Protection

You have shown me worlds
Others only dream about
Your expressing of love for me is
Embodied in movies others see
You have done all this
And so much more
Behind the confines
Of those metal doors

In our life together
The depths of our relationship
Has raised to ultimate levels
Our love has been the catalyst
For a deeper sense of learning
A deeper degree of loving

We have that *je* ne sais quoi
You know that special something that
When I think of you
When you think of me
When in each other's company
Admiring the aura of each other
Makes you say *ooh* and me say *aah*

You are
My air
My life
My love
My yesterday

My today
My forever

It is a great thing
To be dependent on each other
We simply cannot live
Without each other
Can't love without the other
Now I can see and understand why
Lonely hearts cause people to die
When their love has been taken away
I know that I could never bear
To live my life without you
I pray that we go home together
So neither has to bear
The heartache of being
The loved one left behind
Do you know how I feel?
Am I wrong to feel this way?
Does anyone feel the way I feel?

The gift of love
One of God's greatest flowers
Bloomed in the witching hour

Who ever said
Flowers don't bloom in the moonlight
Never knew you and me

You never know where you'll find love. That's the surprising thing about it.

It sneaks up on you when you least expect it and when you are the least bit prepared.

It takes your breath away and leaves you wanting more.

It's a feeling that everyone experiences regardless to where it takes place.

—Geo and Anise

Shattering the Myths about Our Relationships

Susan Goins Castro

"… Father, forgive them; for they know not what they do."

—*Luke 23:34*

Nobody has any idea how hard it is to be a prison wife unless you have lived the lifestyle. There are so many days that I wonder how in the world we are going to get through this.

It's not easy being in a relationship when your husband is in a state correctional facility. Many people feel that being the wife of a prisoner is glamorous. Why, I don't understand, because it's far from being that.

Others wonder what is wrong with me. It has to be something wrong that I couldn't find a man out here. Is she overweight? Is she crazy? Does she have low self-esteem? Was she abused as a child growing up? It has to be one of those. What other reason would I marry a man I met while he was in prison? It never crosses their mind that maybe just maybe it had to do with love.

You never know where you may find love. I didn't set out to find it in a correctional facility, but that's what happened, so it is what it is. I never in my wildest dreams could have imagined that my marriage would stir up so much interest in so many people. I've even been approached by people wanting to interview me about my relationship and why it exists, so I decided to set the record straight and tell the story myself.

What people don't seem to understand is that I have a real marriage. The only difference is that my husband isn't home with me for the moment. We didn't have a big extravagant wedding. It took place in a little space outside of the visiting room. There was the judge, a corrections officer, two witnesses and my husband and me.

The fact that our wedding took place at a correctional facility doesn't make it any less special to us. We take the vows that we made that day very seriously. My husband is my best friend. The reason our relationship is as wonderful as it is is because of the great communication we have.

Because of the way we met, we had no choice but to really get to know each other. This was done in all the letters that we wrote and all the phone conversations we had. He and I can talk about anything. We were friends before getting married and we have continued to still be friends.

Many people in society feel that inmates who get involved in these types of relationships are only doing it to have a connection to the outside world. Others feel they do it in order to have a sexual relationship with a woman or to have someone they can use to bring packages, send money or to transport drugs. While this may be true in some instances, this is a practice that takes place every day everywhere, not only in prison.

Everyone hopes to one day be able to meet a person who means the world to them and who will love them for who they are. Just because a person is incarcerated, those hopes don't change.

My relationship with my husband is just as real or in some cases more real than a lot of relationships that aren't separated by the walls of a correctional facility. We have to work at keeping our relationship together every day. There are so many little things people take for granted that my husband and I don't. I feel that our communication is a lot stronger than the average couple because that's what our relationship was built on. Our first date was a phone conversation. Because of the situation, we were forced to rely on verbal and writing skills. We cherish the time that we are able to spend with each other, even if it's in a visiting room.

There is nothing exciting about having a mate in the system. It's a very lonely existence. Everything falls on you and you alone. You have the responsibility of paying all the bills, providing for your children if you have any and in some cases supporting your husband. You have to be strong enough to carry the weight of the world on your shoulders at all times, and there are some days when you are tired of having to be so strong, but you know that the smallest crack will cause everything around you to come tumbling down so you just carry on.

You have little time for yourself because there is always something that needs to be done or someone for whom you need to do something. It's very easy to lose sight of who you are and the things that you want in life.

My husband and I have been married for almost four years now, and I miss him terribly. In the beginning, I thought that this relationship wouldn't be too hard because even though I loved him to death, he and I never had a relationship before he was incarcerated. I thought that the old saying you can't miss what you never had would apply to us but I was so wrong. When things began to get harder for me, I figured, oh, it will get easier as time goes by. Again, I was wrong. It seems as though the more time I spend with him, the more I crave him. Instead of the years getting easier, they are getting harder.

I've noticed that now that the kids are getting older and more involved in different activities, I miss him more. For example, our younger daughter participates in cheerleading. She has done this for a couple of years now and mostly at practices and games, I've only seen mothers. But at the end of each season, the girls go away for competition. It's during this time that I see entire families, and that bothers me at times because it's just me and the kids.

I really began to feel it these last couple of months because our daughter and son were playing basketball. I really missed my husband during this time. All I saw at practices were dads and their kids. I would actually be sad when I was sitting at the games cheering one of the kids on. Then it happened. I just broke down crying at a game. My daughter's team was playing and one of her teammate's fathers went over to give her some advice, and all I could think about was how that should be her dad giving her that advice and cheering her on.

I wonder at times how this is affecting our children. Our seven-year-old is always asking when my husband is coming home. I wonder if they feel the loneliness that I experience at times and if it's fair to them, growing up without him being at home. If you noticed, I didn't say growing up without him. I said growing up without him being home because there's a big difference between the two.

My husband stays as involved as he can when it comes to our children. He keeps up with their grades and how they're doing in school. I send him copies of all report cards and progress reports. He calls home twice a week and speaks to them about the things going on in their lives. We also have family reunion visits to keep the bond of being a family. Many feel that children shouldn't be exposed to such a lifestyle, but I think that it depends on the circumstances.

One thing about this life is that you have to be a very strong-willed person in order to survive. It can easily break you down if you're weak. You face so much opposition in a relationship like this. It has caused me to drift away from a lot of friends who just didn't understand it.

People ask, "What can he do for you in there?" What they fail to realize is that he does so much for me. Things that you receive in life aren't always based on financial rewards. My husband has taught me the true meaning of love. I've also come to realize that my happiness is important, not just the happiness of others. He has helped me to believe in dreams again and to have faith that anything is possible. I've also learned a great deal of patience from him.

I'm so impressed by all the things that he has accomplished. Even though he is currently serving time, he is doing the time, the time isn't doing him. Since he's been incarcerated, he has received his associate's and his bachelor's degree and is planning to begin working on his master's degree shortly—something that we are paying for since educational funding for inmates was cut out of the budget some years ago. He plays a very active role in many different organizations within the facility and is also a peer counselor to new inmates coming into the system. He is preparing himself for the day that he comes home because he has goals and dreams he wants to achieve.

What people fail to realize is that he made a mistake—something that happens every day because no one is perfect. In life, the most important thing is to learn from your mistakes so that you don't repeat them. If I didn't feel that he had learned from his, I wouldn't be involved with him.

This situation has taught me not to be so critical and judgmental of others. I have to admit that this is something I have to work on daily but I do try. Nobody has the right to pass judgment on another individual. Yet we do this every day.

I don't want my husband to be judged on his past mistakes. I'd rather people meet him and then make a decision based on the man standing before them. Because of these reasons, I really don't discuss my husband. I find that it's easier this way. Don't misunderstand that last statement. I never deny my husband or my marriage. It is what it is and regardless of what people think or say, our relationship is here to stay.

I often wonder why people are so fascinated by a relationship or a marriage that takes place while one of the parties involved is incarcerated. Many say how can there be monogamy in relationships such as ours. You have many couples who practice monogamy as I'm sure there are many couples who don't practice it. This happens in the outside world also. Everyone has his own set of rules when it comes to this, I guess. As for me, I just always try to look at things from his perspective, thinking what if the situation were reversed. What would I expect and want from my husband or how would I feel if he were to get involved with someone else even if it was only for sexual gratification?

Now this is a question I hear a lot from people who know my situation. They always want to know how I do it. Don't I miss being with a man? My response to them is that I don't miss the touch of a man. I miss the touch of my husband. Sex isn't only a physical act. It involves becoming one with another person on a spiritual and emotional level. It's a matter of connecting totally with that person.

My husband and I are able to incorporate sex into our relationship because of the family reunion program, which allows married couples and family members to have forty-four hours of private time together on the grounds of the facility. The purpose of this program is to help keep families together during the time that a member is incarcerated. This gives you a chance to enjoy one another's company without having an officer looking over your shoulder. This helps out tremendously.

Not everyone can participate in this program. There are many states and facilities that don't allow it. What correctional facility decision makers and lawmakers need to understand is that this program does a lot as far as keeping the rate of violence down. Inmates who participate in it are a lot less likely to get into trouble for fear of losing the privilege of being in the program. I'm not sure if there has ever been a study based on this but there really should be.

I'm thankful that my husband is at a facility that participates in the program, but there are many women out there who are not as fortunate. There are a lot of women who marry men who aren't allowed these privileges. You also have many women who marry men who have no chance of ever coming out of prison and others who have been sentenced to death row. Most of us do what we do for the same reason: love.

When I first began this life with my husband, it was a very lonely existence. I didn't personally know anyone else who was going through this. I used to search the Internet looking for some type of support group for people with family members who were incarcerated. Finally one day in 2004, I came across a website that offered just this. I was so excited to find other people who were experiencing this and who could understand what I was feeling. I have been a member since that day and have recently become a staff member. I have met so many wonderful and supportive people since becoming a member. It's so refreshing to have people with whom you can share this because you need that when you are dealing with the loneliness and isolation this way of life can sometimes bring. I have started some wonderful new friendships with women that I've met on the site.

I was so happy to find something that said something positive about relationships like ours. This was a pleasant change because all the media reports is the negative things that come out of a relationship like this. You can always catch a program on MSNBC, *Prime Time* or *Dateline* about women who marry men who are incarcerated. They only discuss the ones who have gone bad, never the ones who have lasted for years or who have lasted even once the person has been released. Instead, they concentrate on the women who want to marry or who have married a serial murderer or sexual predator. Not everyone in prison is there because of those crimes. They never interview the woman whose husband is in for a drug charge, robbery or maybe even a white-collar crime. They find the person with the worse charge and then want to interview the wife if she got married while he was incarcerated. The media then tries to paint the picture that this is how every woman involved with an inmate is. When this takes place, all inmates and their spouses are lumped into that same category.

Another thing that tends to happen a lot to the spouse of an inmate is that the spouse is looked upon negatively. For example, I once had a person ask me what kind of woman would get involved with an inmate and expose her children to him. My reply to her was that whatever happened involving my husband was in the past and that he is paying dearly for that mistake. It isn't a reply that many people can understand but then again, most people don't understand my relationship in the first place.

I'm not going to be made to feel as though I have to defend my marriage. I married my husband because he touches my heart and my soul. Besides, it's no one's business.

I am a very intelligent and beautiful woman. I hold down a very good job and provide for my family. I went to high school and college, and I'm currently enrolled to further my education. The drive that I have is because of the way I was brought up and just from knowing what it is that I want out of life and how to go about getting it. I'm no fool. I have book smarts and street smarts so I know what it takes to succeed in life. I had a very happy childhood. I grew up in a two-parent home. My mother was an early education teacher, and my father worked for a state agency. I had everything I could ever want for while growing up. I took ballet classes, swimming lessons, piano and flute lessons. I was a girl scout and attended church. I didn't grow up feeling unloved. There was an abundance of it in my home. I am an only child so I received my parents' full attention. My children are being raised the same way because that's what I know. I was never in a situation where I felt that I had to look for love or attention, which is what many feel is the reason for my current relationship. My family, those who know about us never had anything negative to say about the situation. The only people about whom I was concerned as far as having something to say were my parents and my children anyway. I allowed my children to make their own decision about him while explaining to my parents how I felt about him. My husband earned my respect and trust as well as that of our children, which is the reason for him being in our lives.

Prison is supposed to be a place for rehabilitation but instead of helping people to correct their past mistakes, it has become a place for big business. How can you expect a person to come out of prison and fit into society if you haven't given him the skills necessary to get a job and survive? The result is that many people get caught up in the revolving door of the correctional system.

I honestly feel that the reason society has so many questions, thoughts and ideas about what goes on as far as a relationship with an inmate is because it's something that seems to be a mystery. It's the unknown that makes people curious. It's a natural instinct for humans to be nosy. They love to hear about subjects that are edgy or controversial. Prison relationships happen to be a hot topic. There's also the fear of the unknown, which drives people to probe.

Many people out there have been lucky enough to not have a direct connection to the correctional system, so it makes it that much harder to understand these relationships. When I say a direct connection, I'm not only referring to a spouse. I'm referring to a family member or a good friend.

My relationship with my husband began as a simple friendship. I met him through someone I knew. It never crossed my mind that it would turn out to be more than a friendship. He never put any pressure on me to have a relationship with him or tried to pick me up so to speak with empty promises and broken dreams. He was just a good friend. He never once has asked me for money or to send him a package. He also has never asked me to risk my freedom by trying to smuggle in drugs. We are striving to attain the same common goals, and they are living a comfortable life and raising our children together.

I've realized during this process that there is always going to be someone who has something to say about the way a person is living their life, even when it doesn't affect them directly or indirectly. This is something that will never change. I've learned that the key to happiness is being able to overlook things like that, which is what I plan to do from here on out.

My main goal with this piece was to show that we are all human beings. We come in many different colors and with many different backgrounds, but in the end we are all the same. We share the same types of thoughts, feelings, hopes and dreams when it comes to love. I treasure my relationship and marriage as much as you treasure yours.

You never know what life has in store for you, so never say never. I didn't seek out love in a correctional facility. I'm just a girl who fell in love with a boy. And it is what it is ...

Afterword

This project started out exposing our reality of prison relationships and along the way turned into the beginning of a wonderful new friendship. We, three amazing women have not only become co-authors but also good friends. We have shared an abundance of laughs, love and hard work the last few months, and it has been an honor and a pleasure experiencing this time together.

We have shown that love is love. It really doesn't matter where it originates or the circumstances surrounding it. In the end, you can't fight the way you feel about someone when it's meant to be, and we all are meant to be.

There comes a time in life when you have to ask yourself if it is better to settle for someone's empty physical presence or if it is better to live the rest of your life in happiness knowing that the man of your dreams loves you with all of his heart and has the utmost respect for you. We choose the latter.

Love,

Peace and blessings.

978-0-595-42109-1
0-595-42109-1